No Tribes Beyond Us

Francis Isaac

Orange Street Books

The Brilliant World

"In twenty thirty-five, experimental chemist, Vishal V. Vohra, distilled the final version of a compound he had been working on for some time. The substance, C47, while created from common raw materials was time-consuming to manufacture, difficult to refine and almost impossible to set into usable components that would allow its fundamental property to be utilized…"

Cameron entered the kitchen, rubbing his eyes, "…the near lossless conversion of solar energy into electrical power." He fell into a chair at the table his family were seated at and finished the passage for his sister. "The world would never be the same again."

"Time?"

"Nine:fifty-five. You win."

"Of course, I win."

Cameron's gaze swept between his father and his rising mother but the answer he was seeking came from across the table.

"Dad didn't think you'd be up before ten." Tayler lowered her text book, his old school text book and peered at him. "I suppose you're, sort of, up."

"Be kind, sweetie, he is up and ready for the day. Want some toast, honey?"

"Thanks, mom. Is no one going to compliment me on my amazing memory?" To one side of him he heard the oven door open and close and, on the other, his father sipped at his coffee and told Tayler to continue reading. "I guess not." A warm plate arrived on the table before him and he felt a hand rubbing his back.

"Do you remember Mrs. Ross? You met her at nana and grandpa's anniversary."

"No. Who is she?"

"A friend of your nana's. She lived in Bethel until yesterday. Now she's in a retirement village."

The toaster chimed and his mother moved away, leaving Cameron bemused but wary. After eighteen years in this house he knew when something was coming. He looked over at his at his dad who was still drinking coffee and listening to Tayler read. His mother arrived back at the table with some toast and sat down. The tension was beginning to disturb him.

"Okay, what is happening here?"

"What do you mean, honey?"

"Dad?"

"Your grandmother volunteered us to help out Mrs. Ross."

Cameron turned to his mother. "You said she moved out yesterday?"

"There's one room left to clear. Nana called last night, I would have told you about it then but you got in so late. She said you can keep anything you like from the room; it's just got to be cleared. House has already been sold."

"But I'm on holiday?"

"You're not on holiday, honey."

Cameron gawped at his mother. By now Tayler had stopped reading and was watching the live drama unfolding in front of her.

"School broke up yesterday. It was my last day, it's summer."

"It's Saturday." Cameron was confused. "You never go to school on Saturday so how can it be a holiday? The holiday starts on Monday when you would be at school... or have classes as it will be."

Cameron heard his father stifle a chuckle and realized that as far as his parents were concerned this was a done deal. He found his little sister's eyes and nodded at her. "I hope you're paying attention." At his words, the room filled with raucous laughter from both ends of the table.

Mr. Herrick was first to compose himself. "It's a good deed, Cameron. You should get in as many as you can before college."

* * * * *

Mr. Herrick had booked an auto pick-up for the day but they had to walk into the city center to collect it. In another town, the vehicle's self-drive function would have delivered it to the curb outside their home but in certain Waterbury neighborhoods, residents had been known to take pot-shots at empty autos.

The way was all downhill and, as they walked, Cameron looked over the gleaming panel-covered roofs of the buildings further down. He could still, just about, remember the view before them; that dull world where power was delivered beneath the ground or through cables held high by ugly frames and not captured directly from the sun and provided, virtually, free to all.

"How's your head?"

3

"It's okay."

"Glad to hear it. Because you smelt like a brewery when you came in last night."

Cameron took a moment to consider his reply. "I think some of the guys had some beers where we ended up." His father hummed and said nothing further. "I thought you were both asleep?"

"We were, once you got home. I guess, come September, there'll be no more of that. That'll be different."

"I'll be home at the end of every term, dad."

"Yeah."

The Subah Corporation, the organization that manufactured, distributed, installed and maintained the rooftop panels was, by some distance, the largest employer in the world. There was a high-security factory, the size of a large town, in northern India that operated twenty-four hours a day, seven days a week and fifty-one weeks a year to produce the finished panels to the exact shape and size ordered by the Corporations' surveyors.

In the fifteen years since the creation of C47, Subah had removed energy costs from most of the global economy. Working under a unique U.N. mandate, it supplied its technology to the private homes and commercial properties of its subscriber nations and, in the process, had super-charged battery innovation, ended world drought with its solar-powered irrigation systems and illuminated a clear path to ending climate change.

There were, of course, some holdouts but they were fewer every year. Untold governments and private companies had tried to replicate C47. None had come close. And then there were the old Petro States who refused to shift from their economic model in any way. They still had a market supplying the world's militaries who Subah refused to deal with. Cameron wasn't looking to relocate to the sub-continent but the Environmental Studies degree he would begin in the autumn would set him up for any number of positions within the Corporation.

Within Connecticut the auto powered father and son down the highway. Mr. Herrick sat up in the driver's seat behind a wheel that remained motionless as the auto switched lanes; his feet nestled beside static pedals as they accelerated and decelerated. He had learned to drive in an actual car and retained the need to be ready to take manual control at any moment. Cameron, from a reclined position beside him, watched his father's eyes move between the auto's displays and the road ahead. 'He's stuck in his time,' Cameron thought and wondered if this would happen to him one day.

"The room belonged to her daughter. She moved out of it years ago but Mrs. Ross kept it as it was for when she visited. Then when she died, she couldn't bear to change it."

"The daughter? How?"

"Climbing accident. Your mother knew her a little; said she was that type of girl." His voice began to trail off, "Terrible. So young."

"Okay. I suppose it is a good deed."

"That's the spirit."

The auto exited the highway and began its start-stop progress through town streets. Cameron knew they were in Bethel when overhanging branches started to block out the sky. He straightened up his chair and looked around. They were on a cul-de-sac rolling up to the last house. It stood alone and backed onto a wood. All the curtains were drawn.

5

The auto parked itself and sounded a loud chime to let them know they had arrived but Mr. Herrick wasn't satisfied. "I'm going to turn us around and back onto the sidewalk. No point doing more carrying than we need to.

"Go inside and check out the room, it's on the first floor. Keys under the mat."

"Really?"

"Really."

Cameron climbed out and walked up to the house. It was warm day so he had settled on a threadbare t-shirt and some old jeans knowing he was going to get dirty but, being on such a nice street, he felt a little out of place now. Back the way they had come, a neighbor had appeared on their porch to watch them. They smiled and waved at him. He returned the wave with as innocent a manner as he could manage before stooping to lift the doormat. The key was there as promised.

The interior was empty yet still smelled of life. Cameron jogged upstairs and looked around. There was only one closed door. He stepped up to it, turned the handle and pushed it open.

He felt the change immediately. Even fully furnished this room had a stillness very different from downstairs. The bed had been made and hairbrushes sat ready on a spotless dresser; simply to look at it, the occupant might have just popped out to return later. Cameron knew better, of course, and there was no telling how much that foreknowledge informed his other senses of the indefinable absence they registered, making all he was seeing around him feel slightly unreal. Almost fake.

Mr. Herrick arrived in the room with a roll of bin bags. "We'll start with the heavy stuff, the wardrobe, the bed, and then take care of the rest of this." He knelt by the bed and threw back its covers to examine its construction. "Okay, this is a problem."

"What is it?"

"We're going to need some tools to take this apart and I didn't bring any." He stood and tossed the roll of bags onto the bed. "I'm going to knock on some doors, ask the neighbors. Empty out the wardrobe, those drawers and start bagging up."

Cameron opened the wardrobe's double doors, began grabbing armfuls of clothes and depositing them on the bed. Once the rail was empty he commenced deconstructing a wall of shoeboxes at the bottom of the closet, clearing the floor of the interior and revealing a strange mark. He took out his phone, activated its torch and squatted to take a closer look. It wasn't a single mark at all but a very faint arc-shaped scratch. Cameron traced its line with a finger to the back panel of the wardrobe and a loop of plastic poking out from behind it. Curious.

He stood and edged his way around the side of the wardrobe and then returned and examined within. There was a significant gap between the actual rear of the cabinet and the shiny panel that bounded its internal dimensions. Cameron rapped at it with a knuckle and listened to the sound. Curious, indeed. He walked over to the window and looked down at the cul-de-sac. There was no sign of his father.

Back at the wardrobe, Cameron lifted the clothes rail from its brackets and tossed it onto the bed. He knelt and threaded a finger through the small loop. The panel jerked and then slid evenly, its edge tracing the same arc in the interior's base that he had observed earlier and revealing something he doubted even Mrs. Ross, the previous owner of this property, had been aware of. He raised his phone and lit the items nestled within the hideaway.

On the floor there was a Polaroid. It was a quartet of young people, three men and a woman smiling at the camera. They looked like college buddies. The feel of it was strange in his hand. Though it had likely been hidden here for years, its back retained a smooth gloss while the image had hardly faded. He couldn't remember the last time he had seen a hardcopy photograph, nevermind handled one. The second artifact was something Cameron was sure he had never seen or touched before but he knew what it was.

The front door and the sound of feet climbing stairs reached him from outside. He slipped the Polaroid into a pocket, pushed back the panel and closed the wardrobe's doors. It clicked shut just as his father entered the room and held up a lumpy plastic bag.

"Got 'em. Let's get this done."

"Dad, before we start, I think I'd like to keep this wardrobe."

Cameron swerved his father's bewilderment at his desire for another wardrobe when he had a perfectly good one in his bedroom and distracted him with an enthusiasm for the job at hand which delighted and surpassed the senior Herrick's expectations. Soon the room was clear and the back of the pick-up loaded with the last of the old occupant. Cameron took one last look around before heading downstairs, locking up and posting the keys through the front door's letterbox. His father, having returned the borrowed tools, was already behind the wheel of the auto and now insisted on taking control of the fully laden transport.

He drove them first to a transfer station where they unloaded everything bar the wardrobe in the corner set aside for recycling. And then to a Goodwill where they dropped off half a dozen bags of clothes before merging with the highway back to Waterbury. On the road home, Cameron, once again, reclined his seat before activating the privacy mask on his phone's browser. Its searches were mostly met with warnings and a few with links to places he didn't think he wanted to go but one site seemed promising.

Skyline Magazine. It had ceased publication nearly a decade ago but its ten issues had been archived and the site still listed an email for the editor. Cameron composed a short message and sent it.

"D'you want me to follow you into town with our auto? We can ride it back home."

"You think your dad can't manage the walk up the hill? I'm not that old."

"That's not why," Cameron protested. "Just makes sense."

"I'll be fine. Text Tayler and tell her to ask your mother if she wants me to bring anything back."

"Why don't I just text mom?"

"Because she doesn't live with her phone in her hand like the two of you."

He sent the text.

Soon they were back in Waterbury and his father was turning the pick-up around while Cameron opened the garage door. Tayler came out as they were carrying the wardrobe inside.

"What is that?"

"What does it look like? It's a wardrobe and it's mine so don't touch it." They set it down in the back and straightened it.

"Mom says get some fresh tomatoes."

"Did she say how many?"

"I don't think so." Tayler joined her brother in front of the wardrobe while their father left the garage. "Why do you want a dead girl's wardrobe?"

"She wasn't a girl. She was older than me. Mom told you the story?"

"Canyoneering. She said her and her boyfriend both died. And now you've got a piece of her old furniture."

Cameron turned to her. "What if I told you it was haunted?"

"A haunted wardrobe?"

"Anything can be haunted." As he spoke he reached an arm around her back. "A ventriloquist's doll, a musical instrument, a piece of jewelery you put on a chain and hang around your..." He brought a clawed hand down on Tayler's far shoulder. She yelped and jumped back.

"You're a jerk."

*   *   *   *   *

Cameron awoke and looked around his room. The curtains were not fully closed and there was light enough to see everything in its place which made him wonder what it was he was looking for. He reached under his pillow and pulled out his phone. Its display told him that it was five:forty-one, the earliest he could remember being up for some time, before the tapping that had disturbed his sleep started up again.

He threw off his covers and followed the sound over to the window and a looming figure he could now make out on the other side. Cameron pulled back the curtains and the silhouette was replaced by a young man, only a little older than him, in a pair of smart-goggles. As if it were the most normal thing in the world, Cameron opened one of the side-windows.

"I'm told you have something to sell?"

"Sure. Meet me out front by the garage. I'll switch off the alarm."

The stranger nodded and then drifted back from the window, still twelve feet above the ground, before gliding in a descending crescent around the side of the house.

Cameron made his way down the conventional way, taking care to avoid every squeaky stair and creaky foot of floor he could recall. He entered the garage through the internal door in the ground floor hallway and pulled up the exterior one to find the stranger waiting. He had dismounted his air-board which now hovered beside him with a gentle hum. Cameron beckoned him inside and the board followed its rider.

"Call me Imp. And you would be Cameron Herrick?"

"I am but I didn't put my address in that email. How did you find me?"

"You're the only 'Cameron Herrick' in Waterbury and this is the closest big town…"

"City." Cameron corrected him. "Waterbury's a city."

"If you say so. The cell-tower the mail was sent from is right at this 'city's' limits."

"You traced that?"

"Wasn't hard. Believing you'd use an account with your real name? That was hard."

Cameron was a mite insulted but, as he had an inkling this was his guest's intent, he hid his offence so as to deprive Imp of any satisfaction while he led him over to the wardrobe. The sooner they could conclude their business the better. The board followed, obediently, a few feet behind. It truly was a remarkable piece of engineering and far more impressive in action than the static, hidden model Cameron now revealed.

The smart-mouth fell open and, behind his goggles, Imp's eyes lit up. He reached into the wardrobe and, carefully, extracted the air-board, laying it on the floor and running his hand across its surface.

Cameron observed that both boards were of the same design. Three enclosed circular rotors within concentric housings were fitted, in sequence, down the length of the body with bindings for the rider's feet fixed either side of the central rotor. Almost every other square inch of the surface had been coated with a clear resin to protect the sparkling, granular C47 that made airboards the illegal items they were. They owed their very existence to black market waste from a time before Subah had optimized its production process.

From one of the pockets of his baggy cargo pants, Imp produced a instrument Cameron had never seen before and directed it at different parts of the board. A small digital display on the tool produced a series of numbers that made its wielder smile before he remembered himself and became serious again. Imp stood.

"Well, it's genuine. I'll give you five thousand dollars for it."

Imp reached into another pocket and produced a fanny-pack, holding it out to Cameron. Five thousand had been far more than he had been expecting, nevertheless Cameron felt their interaction, up to this point, warranted a moment of silence. It was a moment Imp filled in quickly.

"You won't get a better price and if you try selling it elsewhere you might get arrested. Five grand. I'll wait while you count it."

Cameron put him out of his torment. "Deal." And snatched the pouch from his hand.

As promised, Imp stood by as he counted out five banded wads of hundred dollar bills and then, at Cameron's nod, mounted his board and carried the other off with him into the sky. Cameron closed the garage door behind him and walked back into the house. It was still quiet. Upstairs in his room, he climbed back into bed with the fanny-pack and pulled his duvet over both of them.

He awoke a few hours later with the sun fully up. On his way to the bathroom he could hear his family downstairs and, a short while later, joined them to find Tayler reading from another book. After pouring himself a glass of orange juice and listening for a while he asked after the text.

"Ancient history. It's all translated from Latin. That's why it sounds funny."

"When do we get to the fighting?"

"Dad, he's trying to establish peace. It's a carrot and stick approach."

"I know. I was just expecting a little more stick."

"Is this on your syllabus?" Cameron asked.

"It doesn't need to be." Mrs. Herrick retorted. She was a teacher who had taken a decade-long break to raise her children; the eldest of which she now directed a disapproving glare at. "You can learn simply for the pleasure of learning. We may have a future historian in the house."

"A future historian and a teenage antique lover." Mr. Herrick added. "When are we going to swap out these wardrobes? We can't just leave that thing in the garage."

Everyone turned to Cameron. He had not been expecting this question.

"I don't think I want it anymore."

"Excuse me?"

"I took another look at it and I don't think it fits my room. I'm gonna call the city today and arrange a bulk collection for Monday. I'll pay for it."

"So you wanted it yesterday but now you don't?" Mrs. Herrick stirred her coffee and spoke in a measured tone. "That's what you're saying?"

"Yeah. Maybe it looked different in the light in that room." This wasn't working out. He stood up. "I'm going to put some jeans on and take it out to the curb now. Dad, finish your breakfast, I'll just walk it out."

Cameron left the kitchen and ran upstairs to his bedroom where he managed to rip a small hole in his pajama bottoms in his eagerness to remove them. Bouncing down again, he found the internal door to the garage already open and entered. His mother was standing before the wardrobe. Its doors were wide and her arms folded.

"What was back here?"

"Nothing. We took out all the clothes."

"Don't treat me like I'm stupid. There's a secret compartment back here and there are scratches along the top and bottom. Something was hidden here. What was it?"

"Okay, mom, it's not a big deal…"

"Was it drugs?"

"What? No."

Mrs. Herrick raised her voice to call past him and shortly her husband arrived in the garage and joined her in front of the wardrobe. "Cameron was about to tell me what was back here."

"It was an air-board." His parents reacted with dismay. "It's gone now. I sold it." And every word seemed to make things worse for them.

"Are you insane? You know those things are illegal. You should have called the Fire Department or Subah as soon as you found it. You know that."

"Of course he knows it. But instead of doing that you tricked me into bringing it back here. Into our home. Have you any idea how dangerous those things are?"

"Dad, no, it's not like that. You should have seen this guy who picked it up. He was on his own board and it was like it was part of him. It was following him around and everything."

Mr. Herrick was shaking his head. "Do you know how many kids died on those things?"

Cameron was dumbstruck. He knew very little about the air-boy craze that had bloomed briefly when he was much younger. He had assumed it just another subculture lost to history and its few remaining enthusiasts, harmless buffs. His parents' reaction now suggested a different, darker story.

"I don't want to know how much you got for it and I don't want you to bring anything you buy with that money into this house." Mr. Herrick left the garage without looking at his son. Behind him, his wife's expression had cooled from shock, through anger to a sadness that disturbed Cameron even more than the other two.

"Your father was a field engineer when kids started dropping out of the sky on those things. He probably went to some of the locations, reporting."

"Mom, I…" She held up a hand.

"I am disappointed in you, Cameron, but I'm going to choose to believe you did this out of ignorance and not greed." She began to walk to the door. "I think its best we don't speak about it again."

Cameron was alone in the garage. It was a loneliness that remained with him throughout the day even as he sat to eat with his family. He emerged from that isolation only briefly when Tayler had knocked on his door to ask him what was going on between him and their parents. He told her he couldn't talk about it and it was half-true. The time he had spent trying to research flyers and the dangers of their boards had been frustrating.

Deaths were mentioned but there were no numbers and there was very little footage of air-boys actually in flight, which was strange. The accidents were attributed to reckless flying, bad engineering and faulty integration of the C47 power source. All credible causes and reason enough, Cameron supposed, for his parents, who would have observed this dangerous amusement come and go, think ill of any role he might take in perpetuating it.

He shooed Tayler out of his room, alluding to a 'situation' which he was going to take care of, then started packing enough clothes for a few days away.

* * * * *

Cameron arrived at the out-of-hours gate of a hire shop as the sun was rising. This time yesterday he had been standing at the window of his bedroom speaking to a stranger on a flying board. Now he was about to travel to New York City to try and find him again. He couldn't be sure that's where Imp was but his accent implied the metropolis which was also the home to Skyline. The defunct publication whose editor he had contacted again before leaving home.

Cameron presented a bank card and his thumb at a scanner, initiating the rumbling of heavy mechanical platforms and ramps which soon delivered a fully charged auto to the gate. It rolled itself out alongside him and, almost immediately, he was disappointed. Scrolling through the hire shop's app last night, his finger had hovered over faster, flashier vehicles multiple times before he moved on, reminding himself that he was on a mission to return money not spend it. And once he had reclaimed the item he had discovered and immediately sold, he would dispose of it as he should have in the first place.

"New York City, New York."

The auto moved off and Cameron felt a sense of peace move through him now he was on his way and certain of his path. He pulled out his phone and tried to switch it into dark-mode only for the phone itself to protest. The device's onboard A.I. informed him that it had noted a number of uncharacteristic behaviors recently and asked how he was feeling.

"I'm fine."

A second question flashed up, asking Cameron if he wanted to speak to someone.

"I don't want to speak to anyone. Go into dark-mode."

This time the device complied, disconnecting itself from the cellular network until he prompted it to reengage.

"I know what I'm doing."

Debts

Gillian was watering her plants when the doorbell rang and, having filled her small apartment with potted, basket-hanging and window-boxed fauna, this was no small task. Some were gifts brought up by friends and family; some she had purchased herself on visits home and one, the most beloved, was a prickly survivor that had traveled with her since her teens and held on through dorm-life, shared spaces and an unhappy couple of weeks of sofa crashing. She ignored the doorbell and continued to do so when it rang again.

The strangers were persistent and leaned into the bell for a longer more irritating ring. Their resolve raised a question in Gillian's mind. Most would have given up and moved on by now as the only noise she could hear within the space was the trickling of water into soil. At the fourth ring she put down her jug and approached the apartment's front door.

Without, in the hallway outside, were a man and a woman. She was younger, thirty-ish, and both were smartly dressed. Even through the distortion of the spyglass it was clear to Gillian they were some kind of law enforcement. She opened the door.

"Gillian Tapp?" The woman asked.

"Yup."

She reached into her coat and pulled out her ID. "I'm Special Agent Mia Burgis and this is Peter Lonkar, Subah external security. Can we come in for a chat? I promise not to take up any more of you time than is strictly necessary."

Gillian moved back and allowed them to enter. "How did you know I was in here?"

"We didn't," Burgis replied. "But the Bureau isn't used to giving up so easily."

She said it with a smile. One that seemed genuine. Gillian wondered if they taught that sort of thing at Quantico.

"I'm hardly John Dillenger. I'm a nobody who works in a big box store and minds her own business."

"You're also the editor of Skyline." The smile disappeared. "I think you can probably guess why we're here. Tomorrow, Noel Lawrence arrives ahead of the award ceremony..."

"Do you have pets, Agent Burgis?" The visitor shook her head. "Good. Still, you might wanna take half a step away from that Blue Glow."

Burgis looked down to a large pot on the coffee table beside her and the rosette of red-edged, fat leaves bursting forth. The most extended of the pointy tips were brushing her trouser leg. She repositioned herself and began again. "No one knows the flyer community like you. We've already tried, unsuccessfully, to open lines of communication with them and now I'd like to ask for your help."

Gillian sighed. "Another award." She walked between her visitors to retrieve the jug and resume watering her plants. "To go along with the Nobel, the Knighthood, Legion of Honor, Medal of Freedom, Order of Merit, Gokha, General San Martin..."

"He's an important man. This world owes him and Vishal Vohra a great deal and I would hope that you, like me, would want to see him enjoy a safe stay while he's in our country."

"You think flyers are a danger to Noel Lawrence? You've got that the wrong way around."

"I'm sorry?"

"I can't help you, Agent Burgis. And the air-boys are gone. They've been gone for nearly a decade."

"Not all of them. We know there's been a gathering in this city in the last couple of weeks."

"You mean he's told you."

Both women looked at Peter Lonkar who had been standing quietly, listening to the back and forth. He cleared his throat.

"Ms Tapp, I know, Horizon, is in New York. All I am asking for is a meeting; just me and him, at a time and place of his choosing. It is a simple message for you to pass on."

"Just you and him? Really?"

"I give you my word.

"He and his friends have questions. I will do my best to answer them. My goal here is simply to see this visit pass without incident. You know Sir Lawrence is retiring at the end of this month. This will be his final overseas engagement as CEO of the Subah Corporation. If my word isn't good enough, then my wish not to see this trip become a circus should assure Horizon I can be trusted."

"But you already know what he wants: access to Subah's archive to find out what happened. It's all they've ever wanted."

Burgis stepped forward. "You must know how ridiculous that sounds? Even if such a database existed…"

"It doesn't," Lonkar interjected.

"… To allow a bunch of, I'm sorry to say this, petty thieves and vandals to root around in the mainframe of the most important non-governmental organization on Earth. It's absurd.

"Now, Ms Tapp, from what I know about this modern crop of flyers, they're all pretty young. I think they need a grown-up to help them make the right decision. To steer them away from crazy conspiracy theories, at the very least."

"You're assuming I don't believe those theories too."

The special agent's eyes communicated her disbelief more powerfully than any words. They searched Gillian's face for any sign of humor and then turned to Lonkar who simply shrugged.

"In different circumstances I might find your naivety sweet but in an FBI agent, it's more worrying than anything."

"Is that right?" Burgis pulled out her ID wallet and extracted a business card. "I'm going to leave this here."

"You really think you're in charge? You're just here to open doors and introduce him." She nodded at Lonkar. "Where Subah goes, Subah is in charge because they can switch the lights off. They can do it any time they want."

"And why would they do that?"

"Why won't they tell the truth about The Fall?"

Burgis turned away and walked to the front door. She opened it and made a point of holding it open as she spoke to Lonkar. "Shall we go?"

Gillian waited until he was at the threshold before calling to him. "Mr. Lonkar, you say you just want to talk; did you bring your guy with you?"

"I don't know who you mean."

"The night-flyer. Is he here in the city too?"

Not for the first time Burgis was lost. She looked from Lonkar to Gillian and then back again, hoping for some elaboration.

"Please pass on my message."

Lonkar left the apartment followed by Burgis who closed the door behind them. And Gillian was left to her plants. She still had half of them to water and there could be no return to the leisurely pace she had been enjoying before this visitation. She needed to finish the job now because she had to make a call.

*   *   *   *   *

An even pace and eyes front: such effort to do such an ordinary thing and all on the basis of a suspicion. Gillian suspected Subah were watching her. She saw no one as she locked her front door and descended the stairs of her apartment block. Any observers eluded her also on the street but a professional would be trained to blend in and the crush of the subway would make that even easier. Returning to street-level, a short walk from the retail park where she worked, she wondered if they had gone to the trouble of finding out her schedule. Even if they had, such a regular journey would ring only minor bells.

A supervisor spotted her when she entered the store and queried whether or not today was her day off. It was. She asked them if they had seen Brendan and to send him to the break room if they ran into him on the shop floor.

Had anyone been following Gillian, they might have seen one of her co-workers, now in his civvies, wheeling a large suitcase out to a station wagon. And, if they had, Brendan Calder would have looked like just another customer. A few blocks away he parked in a back alley, opened the rear of his auto and unzipped the case. It was a display model and would need to be returned to the store when he returned from his lunch break. Before that, he had agreed to take Gillian somewhere. She clambered out thanking him but with no further explanation as to why she had needed this odd favor.

* * * * *

The sky overhead was clear and the road, along which she walked, deserted. Still this was the place.

Gillian's first thought had been this patch on the edge of the city was too far out to be of any interest to planners but she saw now, on either side of the empty road through it, semi-developed compounds with concrete floors. Some were enclosed within fencing and some not with the occasional post or low brick wall separating unoccupied space from vacant lot. They dotted the surrounding uneven ground, standing out as the only spots free of knee-high wild grass. Rayo really had sent her to the boondocks.

Just as she began to wonder how long she would have to wait, Gillian heard the sound of a vehicle on the road ahead. A vehicle driving erratically and soon she was able to see why. Buzzing it like giant angry wasps, a trio of flyers were accosting the speeding auto approaching her. All three were carrying baseball bats they were using to smash what was left of an exterior already missing some panels and all its windows. With one final, violent lurch it left the road for a ditch where it came to a very hard stop.

The flyers circled above. Gillian recognized two of them and, when Rayo saw her, she lowered her bat and descended. "Hola. It's good to see you." She dismounted and allowed her board to hover.

At the auto, the other two flyers had landed also and were pulling out the unlucky driver.

"Who is that?"

"A dust-dealer. At least he was. Now we are pretty sure he's an informant."

"'Pretty sure?'"

"Times like these, it's hard to be too careful, Gillian." Rayo pulled up her goggles and rested them on her forehead. "So, Subah made contact?"

"Peter Lonkar. Him and some FBI lapdog yapping at his heels dropped by to see me this morning."

"Lonkar? Deputy Head of Security. They're rattled."

"He wants a sit-down with Horizon. One on one, that's what he says."

"Well, that's not going to happen."

"I agree. It's a terrible idea."

"What about their operative?"

"My guess is he's in the city right now. Noel Lawrence arrives tomorrow. Lonkar would want…"

Rayo turned away abruptly. Further up the road, one of the flyers had moved away from the driver and was updating her through her earpiece. "Fine. Take him for a ride. See if that helps his memory." She watched her companions mount up and take firm hold of the driver before lifting him into the air. He yelped and wailed as they carried him over her and Gillian.

"Who's the other air-boy with Fever?"

"Polaris. He answered the call like the rest of us."

The women watched the flyers and their unhappy passenger recede into the distance in the direction of Manhattan.

"Tell me about this boy from Connecticut."

* * * * *

Gillian ascended the last stair and turned onto her hallway to find Agent Burgis squatting with her back against the wall beside her front door. Burgis rose upon seeing her.

"Something I can help you with Special Agent?"

"I hope so."

"And what would that be?"

"I'd like to know why won't you help us? I don't understand. All I want is to head off any trouble before it starts."

"That might be all you want," Gillian unlocked her door and stepped inside the apartment. "But what about Subah?" She shut the door on Burgis.

"Subah isn't here," The agent called through the door. "I am. On my own. And I'm off the clock so this is my time I'm wasting not the Bureau's." Burgis waited. There had been no footsteps moving away within the apartment so she was certain Gillian was still there. She lowered her voice. "And please don't say 'Subah is everywhere...'" The door opened suddenly and Gillian stood before her. "Because you're not that bonkers."

Burgis located the front room's 'point Nemo' and positioned herself on it while Gillian rounded a counter that separated the kitchen from the rest of the space.

"I'm making tea. Would you like some?"

"Thank you. No sugar for me." She watched her host pull a second cup from a cupboard and busy herself. "So, who is the night-flyer, Ms Tapp?"

"Gillian. And isn't that something you should have asked Peter Lonkar?"

"I did. His answer was vague."

Gillian chuckled. "For a long time I didn't believe he existed. Just an air-boy legend, someone to blame when they wiped out and wrecked their boards but, over the years, I changed my mind about that. The stories were too consistent, the fear was too real.

"He's another flyer. Wears black and flies some advanced type of board that is, apparently, just as powerful at night as it is in the daytime."

"That makes no sense. Air-boards are solar powered."

"No, they can use artificial light but it's a poorer quality light. In the city, surrounded by streetlamps and windows, you can get off the ground on an ordinary board at night. It would just be risky to go too high.

"The night-flyer doesn't seem to have these limitations. He can go as high and as fast as he wants."

"That's why you think he works for Subah."

"Who else could have developed this tech? No one else has ready access to C47.

"For years he's been taking down flyers, all around the world. There weren't many left to start with and now..." Gillian placed two steaming mugs on the counter and took a bottle of milk from her fridge. "That's why the air-boys won't meet your friend. It's a trap."

"So there has been a gathering." Gillian said nothing. "And this, Horizon, is their leader."

"Flyers have no leader. Their entire philosophy is built around freedom. What do you know about Horizon?"

Burgis stirred her tea. "Very little. We believe he's African American. We believe he's from the west coast and that's about it."

"Then you're missing the one thing that matters."

"Which is?"

"The word on the wind says he's the younger sibling of Brink. Sound familiar?"

The name was familiar to Burgis. As preparation for this assignment she had read every archived issue of her host's long-dead fanzine. There was a profile of this flyer in one of them and one of the few things she could remember of it was that he was based on the west coast.

"I was in my third year at Columbia and Skyline was already up and running, so I was known within the community. It was Christmas. I was back home in Phoenix and I heard about this new flyer in California so I traveled up there before heading back east.

"I'd never seen anything like him. He was graceful in the air. The way he moved, it wasn't like any other flyer. It was like he belonged in the sky. And, as I was watching him, I thought to myself: this is the next chapter; this is where the culture is going. This is the future.

"But there was no 'next chapter.' He died in The Fall, like so many others."

Burgis watched Gillian's eyes drop. The recollection of these events still troubled her, that much was obvious. She glanced around the room and then back at her host across the counter.

"He's a link to their past, then. Horizon. Their past and the injury they believe they've suffered. Them and you. You lost your career."

"Four years studying journalism down the drain. The same papers that had been offering me jobs, a month earlier, were publishing editorials denouncing Skyline. They turned me into some Pied Piper luring kids to their doom. Kids. We were all the same age.

"I even got a visit from you people."

"I know. I read the transcript. The agents you spoke to didn't hold you responsible for any of the deaths. They needed information about air-boys and you were the person to come to. You still are." Burgis sipped her tea. "Why is that?"

"What are you asking me?"

"Journalism isn't the only career. You've got a good degree; you could do lots of things but you keep the Skyline site online and your name associated with it. Why haven't you moved on?

"You've been in New York fifteen years and your apartment's filled with desert plants. I might get it if you were a homesick student but you're a grown woman. You could have left all this behind. Unless you do feel responsible for something?"

"Subah is responsible for what happened."

"Any proof of that?" Burgis asked flatly.

"The proof is in the archive. We know it exists.

"You all treat Subah as if it can do no wrong and Noel Lawrence like he's a saint but they are opaque, high-handed and operate, virtually, without oversight. It didn't used to be controversial to see that as dangerous."

"As dangerous as the wars we used to fight over fossil fuels? You sound like a spokeswoman for one of the Petro States."

"More Subah propaganda."

"I wasn't claiming there were any links, I was just…"

"You think Subah will protect us from the misdeeds of our governments?

"All over Africa, regimes used the rollout of C47 to consolidate control over their populations. And no one said a word. Settlements that stood in the same place for a hundred years, abandoned when the old grid was shut down. Another award for Noel Lawrence; another profile of the great man, saving the world on a bank manager's salary.

"Do you know how many books there are on him and Subah? You could fill an entire section in a library with them and they all say Lawrence is an obsessive record-keeper. All the air-boys want is for Subah to tell the truth about what happened because there is more than what they've told us. Told everybody.

"You're a trained detective. How can you not see this?"

Burgis thought about the cooling tea in her mug and was sure that she would need something stronger if she followed Gillian down this rabbit hole. The secrecy, the leader who wasn't a leader, the obsession with Subah; more and more it felt like she was dealing with a cult.

"I don't know what you want from people, Gillian. Subah and the technological revolution it brought have made the world a better place. Even you can't deny that." She pushed her mug away. "I'm holding out my hand to you – it's time to jump off this crazy-train. Work with me and we can keep a lid on things. Even if this night-flyer is in town, if we can keep things quiet during Lawrence's visit, he and Lonkar will probably just leave again. What's wrong with that plan?"

For a moment Burgis thought she might be getting through to her. Then Gillian stepped back from the counter and straightened up.

"I want to show you something." She walked out of the room and a few seconds later returned holding a VR headset and nodded at the sofa across the floor. "Take a seat."

Burgis remained where she was. "What's the show?"

"You want to know about flyers? See what they see and you'll understand them better."

"That's a flight recording? They're illegal."

"They're illegal to make and distribute. They're not illegal to watch." Burgis gave her a look. "Get your phone out and look it up. It's true."

"Gillian…"

"If you're afraid I'm going to pull a piece on you once you've got these on, I could have poisoned your tea."

The women shared a smile. Burgis was sure this was a bad idea but she walked to the sofa and sat down anyway. She had come here to seek her host's help; this seemed to be a test to determine whether she deserved it. Gillian handed her the headset and settled on the sofa beside her.

"Which folder?"

"Hmm, let's go with 'Fever.' Then 'new stuff' and play the first one."

The headset's display responded to the agent's eye movement, conveying her through a series of menus until she was presented with a bank of files. Burgis focused on the topmost until a yes/no box appeared.

Gillian knew what was coming but it was always fun to watch a newbie experience their first flight. Right on cue, Burgis yelped and her arms came out, one hand almost smacking Gillian in the face. Even knowing she was still sitting on a sofa in an apartment block couldn't stop her body reacting to her eyes and ears suddenly telling her she was on an air-board hovering above a city.

Gillian watched the agent try to recover her balance and then jerk back as the recording propelled her forward into a dive. As Gillian recalled, it was almost to street level before banking down a major thoroughfare. The experience elicited a series of 'woah's, increasing in volume, from Burgis. She had now brought her hands out in front of her as if to protect herself from a collision the chronicler of this flight was far too skilled to suffer.

Soon the hands came down. The flyer had leveled out and begun to gain altitude and Gillian was happy to see Burgis relax enough to take a look around.

"Is this Houston?" Gillian leaned in to be heard above the headset's audio and confirmed it. "It's recent too."

After a few more minutes, Burgis brought a hand up to the side of the headset and paused the recording. She lifted the rig and offered it back to Gillian with a long sigh. Augmented and virtual reality exercises had been part of her FBI training but this was something different. Her heart was beating like a machine-gun.

"If I can't fly, Agent Burgis, I don't want to be part of your revolution."

Burgis nodded. "Have you ever done that for real?"

"Longest I ever spent solo on an air-board was about thirty seconds and I almost killed myself. No." Gillian turned the headset in her hands. "When things went bad, most flyers stuck their boards in the attic and got on with their lives. These recordings are mainly for them. It's a way to keep in touch with the culture."

"You're not going to help me, are you?"

"I'd hoped I just had."

Burgis got to her feet. "Thanks for the tea. If you change your mind, I see the card I left this morning is still there." Gillian nodded. "One more thing. You described Brink as graceful in the air. What about his brother?"

"Horizon? He flies like he's angry. Angry all the time."

Burgis let herself out and, as the apartment's front door closed, Gillian eased back on the sofa and cast her eyes out of the room's windows. The sky remained clear but there was a storm coming.

Hostile Challenge

Cameron was beginning to question his judgment. For the second time on his second morning in New York, he had ordered a big breakfast in the local diner. Yesterday it had made sense. He had started out early and, when he reached the city, needed to find a spot for the auto not too far from his cheap hotel so he was hungry when he finally sat down to have something to eat. But the rest of that day had just been waiting and this one had started the same way.

It felt like he was stuck in a spy story; something that might not have been so bad if it wasn't the wrong kind of spy story. This felt like one of the really slow British serials his mother liked where nothing happened and no one said anything for really long stretches. He looked down at his half eaten meal. A big breakfast two days in a row was a mistake when all he was doing was sitting around. If he was made to wait much longer he would have to take up jogging.

He left the diner slightly embarrassed at how much food he was leaving behind and there they were again in his head. The disappointment on his mother's face and the way his father had refused to even look at him when he had left the garage. It had rocked him. For a moment each had acted as if they were sharing their home with a stranger. He needed to turn that around before he left for Storrs. He didn't want to leave under a cloud. As for whether what he had done had really been so bad, he had his doubts.

He stepped into the hotel's tiny elevator and allowed the creaky cabin to carry him up to his floor. In Waterbury he might have expected a view from a fifth storey window but here there were just the ugly backs of other blocks and an empty alleyway. It was an uninspiring vista to be sure and he had already grown accustomed to ignoring it before something caught his eye on this entrance to his room. A sheet of paper folded and taped to the window. Taped to the outside of the window.

"Can't these people use doors?"

The bottom half of the sheet was a rough map and, above it, instructions for him to leave his phone behind and switch off the GPS in his auto. The wait was over.

*   *   *   *   *

The map directed Cameron to a backstreet a few miles away. He maneuvered the auto down it cautiously. This was clearly a space in frequent use. He could hear the rumble of machinery behind a series of large metal doors and steam and the smell of detergent hung heavy in the air; along with a young woman on her air-board descending slowly before him.

She dismounted and pulled some gadget out of a pocket which she held up while approaching the auto. Without a word to Cameron, she circled the vehicle until she ended up back at the passenger side door and then brought a finger up to her earpiece.

"Regreso a casa."

The air-board, which had been idling a foot above the ground, shot up into the sky and disappeared out of sight. When Cameron turned back, the woman was sitting beside him.

"You're the one who found Sprite's board?"

"Sprite? I think her name was…"

"Flyers don't have names, they have call-signs. We knew her as Sprite." She pulled down her seatbelt and secured it. "Let's get moving. I'll direct you."

"To where?" Although this stranger had an accent, Cameron was suddenly very aware that he was the new one in town. "I don't have the money for the air-board on me."

"You don't need it. You think we're dangerous. That you selling us the board is enabling us to harm ourselves. I want to take you to meet our group and, if you feel the same way after that, you can take the board and keep the money."

He only needed a moment to consider the offer. "Okay." And started up the auto. "What's your call-sign?"

"Call me Rayo."

He was grateful he had taken the time to learn how to drive. It wasn't a condition for auto hire in Connecticut but his father had insisted and with the location and navigation functions on this auto off-line, his rusty manual skills were the only way he and his passenger were going anywhere. Rayo sat, mostly silently, next to him, speaking only to guide him to their destination. At her instruction he turned off the populated streets down an empty road with only seagulls overhead for company.

They parked in front of a row of warehouses along an industrialized embankment and got out. Rayo made her way over to one of the buildings while Cameron looked around. This was a working dock once. The scars of industry were everywhere but the merchandise, the machines and the men who operated them were long gone. Behind him he heard Rayo call his name. It seemed only those that took to the air still needed this place.

She was at the door to one of the warehouses. It looked abandoned. As he approached, she pulled it open for him and then followed him inside.

The interior was vast and mostly empty. Overhead, built into a slanted roof, a series of skylights allowed for illumination and ventilation with its open central section connected, via a line of arms and pulleys, to a wheel-turned handle. At various points across the floor, bits and pieces of tech had been dumped seemingly at random. Cameron recognized a number of portable generators among them but the purpose of other components was a mystery to him and still more were covered in tarp. Against one wall, a sofa and a quartet of air-boards rested and, opposite it, a number of workbenches supporting more, partially dissembled, boards and a couple of guys, one of which he recognized.

"It's the wardrobe-kid. Find anymore treasures? Or lost fairytale lands, whatever?"

Rayo took over the introduction. "You know Imp. This is Miguel; he's a friend of ours. Miguel, Cameron."

Miguel was at least a decade older and many more pounds heavier than the flyers. He reached across the bench and shook Cameron's hand. "Did you know Sprite?"

"No. My mom knew her mom. Me and my dad were just clearing out her old room as a favor." Cameron hesitated before continuing. "You do know she's dead?"

"I know," he nodded. "I recognized her board straight away. She used to come down to New York and hang out with a crew that was based in the city back then. She was the only girl-flyer I'd seen until Rayo."

Miguel's eyes were kind but Cameron thought he saw a sadness in them too. Whether it was for times past or for where they all found themselves now, he wasn't sure.

"When we discover an old board," Rayo began, "we reclaim it and, when we find the right person, pass it on. It's a way to keep the community alive. There's no more dust coming out of Subah so there's no way to create new boards. All we can do is try and repair and upgrade the ones already in existence."

"Is that what you're doing here?"

"It is. These are all Sun Jammers, like the board you found. It's the most popular design and easiest to look after. You might have noticed my board looked a little different?"

Cameron shook his head. He had paid no attention to Rayo's board until it had taken off on its own, at which point it was just a blur.

"It doesn't matter. My type of board is called a Clipper, it's optimized for speed. There are other styles too. There's a lot more to our world than they would have you believe."

"I believe you. Look, if it was down to me…" He sounded like a coward. He started again. "My folks know that I sold you the board and it's just created a whole, weird, unpleasant thing between us. They don't understand you guys and they're never going to. And I can't really be dealing with all this right now.

"Imp, I told Rayo I'd gladly give you back the money."

"And what do I do with it? We can make more boards but we can't power them. There's no more dust to be had. She just told you."

"But I can't be a part of this. Trading C47 is illegal, handling it is dangerous. I know that now."

"You want to know what's dangerous?" Imp picked up a small conical-shaped component from the workbench and held it up. "This is a synchronizing power and inclination node drive zoner: flyers call it a 'spindizzy.' It keeps the rotors in an air-board turning at complimentary rates and working together. Do you know what would happen if this malfunctioned in flight?"

"I don't know, man. The board stops flying."

"The board will fly fine but, if you're on it, after ten minutes you'll have micro-fractures in every bone from your big toes to your knee caps. Every flyer knows how to strip one of these down and put it back together. We're a maker culture. We have to be. We can't take our boards down to a showroom and have them tuned-up. We know what we're doing and we know how to fly."

Something must have changed in Cameron's face. "What?" Imp demanded.

"Then why did so many of you die?"

In the silence that followed Cameron heard seagulls calling to each other in the sky overhead. It was the only sound. Then he felt a tap on his arm.

"Walk with me."

Rayo led Cameron over to the sofa and they both sat down. "We call it 'The Fall.' That's what you're talking about even though you don't realize it.

"I wasn't there, of course, I've heard this from different flyers down the years. They all say it started with the dealers. They'd got hold of a new batch of dust, the purest and most refined yet. No one knew what had happened at Subah but no one cared. Instead of fighting over dust, being exploited by the dealers, all of a sudden there was enough for everyone and it was the best quality anyone had ever seen.

"Once dust is set in a casing you can't remove it, so flyers started constructing new boards to take advantage. It was a frenzy of building. People were racing to take to the air. They didn't know what was coming."

She became quiet and another time Cameron might have respected the emotions he saw playing across her face but he needed to know. "What happened?"

"There was a problem with the dust. After seventy hours this batch lost its potency. It stopped being able to convert solar energy, almost completely, and flyers fell out of the sky. All over the world flyers fell out of the sky. The lucky ones only broke bones."

Cameron was shaken. In the background reading he had done there had been no hint of this kind of intrigue yet he was sure Rayo believed it. Even though it was incredible, they all believed it.

An air-boy descended through the warehouse's skylight. He dismounted and walked over to the workbenches to join Imp and Miguel while his board floated towards the sofa. As it came close, Cameron heard its rotors begin to hum at different frequencies, and it tilted itself upwards before resting against the wall alongside the other air-boards.

"It didn't take long for people to work out what had happened. Subah had sabotaged the dust. They had tainted it somehow to make it useless. We don't know if they expected all the deaths but they must have known it was a possibility. Since then we've been trying to force them to admit it."

"Wait… You think the Subah Corporation was behind this?"

"Who else could it be? The dust came from them; it's a by-product of their C47 processing. And they always hated us."

"That's still a big leap. You're talking about manslaughter on a massive scale."

Rayo's tone hardened. "It wasn't manslaughter, it was an atrocity. And the world looked the other way."

Cameron knew better. The world may not have been interested in a spat between flyers and Subah but it was in young people dying. His parents' reaction convinced him of that. This one-sided version of events leading up to the tragedy Rayo had described fitted many of the facts he learned from other sources yet there were too many gaps in it; holes in their knowledge of Subah's actions and the workings of a black market that they had filled in with guilt, anger and grief. She didn't seem to see it.

The newly arrived air-boy was walking over to them. Rayo greeted him as he approached and asked about the wind.

"A few more police drones in the air but that's about it. Everything's looking good for the morning."

"Good. Fever, this is Cameron. He found that last board Imp brought back and now he's deciding whether he's going to let us keep it."

"Why would that be his decision?"

"I gave him my word. Horizon agrees."

The eyes of both flyers turned to Cameron who believed he had been seated long enough. He planted his feet and rose, taking care to make every action obvious and slow.

"I respect everything you've built here, how you take care of each other, and I'm sorry for your loss but I just want to take Sprite's board and leave now." He looked from Fever to Rayo and briefly wondered whether he should offer to return the money again before rejecting the idea. This wasn't about money for them.

Rayo nodded behind him. "The second one on the wall there."

Cameron stepped up to the board and took hold of it with both hands. It was heavier than he had expected and weighted in an unusual way. He let it rest back against the wall and realized that he had never actually handled one of these things before. This air-board was almost as tall as he was, a foot and a half wide, and he didn't want to break it in front of people he knew valued it far more than him.

He reached out again and then hesitated, at which point he was barged aside by Fever who expertly lifted and held the board under one arm.

"That your auto outside?" Cameron nodded. "Let's go."

The embankment was as empty as it had been when he'd arrived. Cameron opened the auto's door, pushed down the passenger-side seat and stood back while Fever inserted the board.

"When I was in her room; her old room in her mom's house, there wasn't much in there that told me who she was. I didn't really think about it at the time but that board, hidden in the back of a wardrobe, it was the realest thing about that space. The most honest."

Fever straightened up and looked at him. "And what do you think she'd want you to do with it?"

"Give it to you. But I can't."

"Dust is a must, hombre. Without it we can't fly and, if we can't fly, we're not flyers. You're helping Subah to end us. If you're going to do it, make your peace with it."

Cameron shook his head. "The way you guys talk about Subah..."

"Kid, I'm sorry to rock your world, but Noel Lawrence isn't Santa Claus and the Corporation are not his merry elves.

"Do you know in every panel, on every rooftop, there's a chip controlling it? They can access it and switch it off with one of their satellites at any moment. Boom! No more power."

"That's for maintenance. Unless you want engineers working on live circuits?"

Fever turned away laughing. "Okay, that's what it's for. Take care, kid." He re-entered the warehouse and the door mechanism locked behind him.

They were a funny group. Cameron guessed from their accents, Imp and Miguel were locals; Fever was definitely from the south and, he was pretty sure, Rayo was Mexican. What were they all doing here together, he wondered, and, as he did, it slowly dawned on him that he had seen Miguel before. He was one of the men in the Polaroid he had found along with the air-board but he looked so different. He looked happy.

The picture was back in Waterbury. He hadn't thought to bring it. In fact, he had forgotten all about it. He got into the auto and powered it up, resolving to find a way to return the snap to the flyers.

"Privacy."

The vehicle's clear windows darkened around him as he reversed onto the dock road. Now he just needed to remember the way back to his hotel. The seagulls wheeled overhead as he departed.

* * * * *

Special Agent Burgis had arrived at the FBI's New York office expecting a quiet morning. Peter Lonkar, who had spent the last few days with them, had left to take direct control of security during Noel Lawrence's visit. The Subah chairman had arrived in the city and would be attending a reception and his award ceremony tomorrow before departing that day. Meanwhile, her team's covert and overt attempts to contact the air-boys had all come to nothing. If they intended to disrupt this visit, as she believed they did, the bureau had very little intelligence to suggest how they might go about it.

While the rest of the team monitored chatter, Burgis took a tablet and found an empty interview room where she commenced rereading every edition of Skyline magazine. These back issues, the most recent almost a decade old, were unlikely to give her any leads on Horizon or his plans but they might shed more light on the flyer mindset. At this point she was certain even the smallest additional insight would be helpful.

Halfway through the review she came to Gillian Tapp's profile of Brink. It wasn't how she remembered it. On second reading it stood out from the other reporting in the magazine for its fluidity and expressiveness. Most of Skyline's writing had the feel of an overworked assignment; it was professional and restrained to the point of becoming technical. The Brink piece was different. It flowed from his start to his personal philosophy and, along the way, related his rumored visit to Europe by, effectively, stowing away on a container ship with a backpack of supplies.

The round-trip had been a pilgrimage to find the Mirror Man. The original flyer who appeared above London, one day in 2037, riding a board coated with shards of C47 panels. Brink refused to say whether a meeting had taken place but Burgis remembered that original flight. She was still at school when video of a man on a flying board had filled the news for days. He was never seen again but eighteen months later the first air-boys started to appear. Their reign would be brief and end with many deaths.

There was a sharp knock and one of her team poked his head around the door. They had got a hit.

Agent Roma, the youngest of the squad assigned to her, explained the target was on the move and, judging by its speed and route, in an auto headed out of the city. Once they were rolling, Burgis put a call into a hub office and passed on the location data. Word came back thirty minutes later that an interception had occurred and local agents, along with a person of interest, were awaiting her arrival on the side of the road. The flyers had got sloppy; probably game-day nerves, and now she had one.

Mindful of the afternoon rush, the Rye office agents had directed the auto off the highway and stopped it on a suburban boulevard. Burgis thought she saw a few curtains twitch when they got out. The residents likely weren't used to this sort of excitement around here. The suspect was younger than she expected and more nervous. She took out her ID and presented it to him.

"I'm Special Agent Mia Burgis. This is Special Agent Theodore Roma. What do I call you?"

"Cameron. Cameron Herrick."

* * * * *

It had taken an hour to take Cameron's statement and he had been sitting alone in an interview room for an hour following that. The starkness of the walls and ceiling, the sterile air being pumped through the conditioning and the constant buzz of the lights overhead all conspired to lull him into a reflective mood and, in that state, he became very aware that there were decisions he had made in the last few days that he now regretted.

The door opened and agent Burgis entered and sat opposite him. She had a folder containing a number of loose pages which she placed on the table before her.

"Cameron, good news. I've managed to confirm most of your story. As, I believe my colleague told you, the more detail you can provide us with the quicker we can get through this…"

"I've told you everything I know."

"Perhaps I can jog your memory. We're still missing a few significant details, like the names of these flyers you interacted with. So far you've only given us one," Burgis consulted her papers, "'Gargoyle.' Who you say came to your home and bought the air-board you found."

"I've tried to remember but they all had these dumb made-up names. They just went in one ear and out the other."

"Gargoyle?" Burgis repeated.

"I think so."

"So, now you're not even sure about that?"

"I'm pretty sure that's what he called himself. I'm sorry I can't be more helpful."

Burgis sat back in her chair and smiled at Cameron. He thought it quite a strange smile.

"Do you follow the news, Cameron?"

"Sometimes."

"Did you know that Noel Lawrence of the Subah Corporation has just arrived in New York?"

"I didn't know that."

"We think the flyers are gathering for some sort of protest." She pushed at the papers in front of her. "But, according to your statement, you didn't overhear anything to indicate what that might be."

Cameron shook his head.

"I understand. Why would they confide in you? You're not an air-boy and you're not ground crew, just a stranger who stumbled into this mess."

"What's ground crew?"

"It's a bit of a catchall term they have for supporters; covers everything from friendly lawyers, who'll represent them, to groupies... who do groupie-things." Burgis regarded him closely. "You're obviously not a lawyer."

"Hey! Hold on." Cameron spluttered. "I'm not a groupie. I only met these people for the first time on Sunday. And then again today."

"And you've already forgotten all their call-signs?"

"Because they don't mean anything to me.

"Look, Agent Burgis, I didn't have to speak to you. I'm trying to co-operate because I have nothing to hide."

"We appreciate your co-operation, Cameron. You're being very helpful."

"No problem. Just as long as we're clear."

"One thing I am not clear about, Cameron, is how a phone we were tracking ended up on the floor of your hired auto?"

"Excuse me?"

"That's how we found you. It was in the well under the passenger seat. It reconnected to the network, in your auto, after being dark for over twenty-four hours."

"I don't know anything about that."

"It belonged to someone we asked to make contact with the flyers on our behalf. Someone they know. They dropped him in a swimming pool."

Cameron shrugged. "Couldn't he swim?"

"It was the rooftop pool of a twenty storey midtown hotel." Burgis leaned forward. "How did the phone get in your auto?"

"I don't know. Maybe it dropped out of her pocket. That's where she was sitting."

"The flyer whose name you don't remember on the way to the warehouse, the location of which, you can't recall?" Cameron remained silent. "You see, what I can't work out is, why they would leave it there on purpose. Did they want you to be caught? They must have known we were looking for it. But, if you're lying to me…"

"I'm not lying to you."

"If you're lying to me, Cameron, then you were taking the phone and that dummy air-board somewhere. For some reason. And I need to know those things."

It took a few seconds for the words to sink in and, as they settled in his mind, he became increasingly uneasy. "That's not a real air-board?"

"No. It's the right weight but it has no working parts and that's not C47. The lab is running tests to find out what it is." Burgis resumed her questioning. "Where were you taking it? Were you supposed to deliver it to someone?"

"I was taking it home. And then I was going to take it to be destroyed, like I should have done with the one I found."

"You can't be that stupid. Why would a flyer hand over a real air-board to be destroyed? Those things are central to their identity.

"Were they paying you?"

"I think I've said enough, Agent Burgis." Cameron sighed.

"Stop talking now and I'll charge you for failing to inform the authorities of the air-board you found in Bethel. And then for giving aid to these flying punks with whatever they're planning to do."

"How do you even know that other board was real? You never saw it."

"I know because we've traced the identity of the girl that lived in that house and she was a flyer. But, if you want to argue that it was a dummy too, you can do that before a grand jury. I hope UConn won't mind you skipping classes to be deposed and attend court."

Cameron felt slightly dazed. Everyone was lying to him and no one was on his side. This FBI agent believed he was working with the air-boys and they, whether deliberately or accidentally, had dropped him into her lap. She was asking him another question but he was finding it hard to focus.

"Cameron, are you listening to me? Was, Horizon, there?"

"No. But they mentioned him. Their names were Imp, Rayo and Fever. Imp was the one who came to my house."

"No one else?"

"No. Just those three."

"What are they planning?"

"I don't know. Fever said something about 'the morning' but that's all."

Burgis checked her watch and then rose. "Come on, we've got to go."

"Go where?"

"To see your friends."

After so long seated, Cameron's knees cracked as he stood, before being hustled from the room. There was a flurry of agents and a blur of corridors before exiting to a bay where Agent Roma opened the front passenger-side door of an auto.

The agent got in beside him and soon Burgis joined them in the back. Night had fallen during his questioning. He tried to lower his window to get a little fresh air but it was locked.

Burgis asked if he needed to start from his hotel to retrace the route to the warehouse. He told her that wouldn't be necessary and guided them and a following vehicle straight to the docks. He was done fighting. Leaving the man with the sad eyes out of his meeting with the flyers was the last of his resistance. The autos rolled past the road to the embankment and turned a couple of blocks down before parking up.

In the rear view mirror, Cameron watched one of the agents in the second vehicle get out and retrieve a large case from their auto's trunk. Within was some kind of stealth-drone which the agent placed on the auto's roof before returning the case and getting back into his vehicle. The drone ascended silently out of his sight but, on the backseat, Burgis was monitoring its camera's live feed. She reported a skylight and lights on within the building and then chided whoever was controlling her eye-in-the-sky not to get too close.

Glare from another pair of headlights temporarily dazzled him. When his eyes returned to normal, another vehicle had joined them and Burgis was handing her tablet to Roma. She got out as a serious looking man from the newly arrived auto disembarked also and the two spoke. On the tablet, Cameron could see that the FBI drone had remained stationary above them and was watching the roof of the flyer's warehouse from two blocks away. He tried to lower his window again, hoping to look up and see it and then remembered he was still in custody.

Outside things were becoming fractious. Burgis and the man had begun arguing, at least she was arguing while he remained calm despite her agitation. Cameron strained to hear what was being discussed but he could barely make out a word before the dispute was over. The man got into his auto and Burgis was hurrying back to theirs mouthing obscenities. Until this very moment he had assumed she was the one calling the shots.

The new auto sped off, turned onto the embankment and began racing for the warehouse. Cameron braced himself as Roma lurched them all forward, in pursuit, with the second FBI auto close behind. Then, in the sky, he saw something moving even quicker than they were: a silhouette against neon lit low clouds descending toward the roof. A flyer on an air-board.

The occupants of the leading auto had already exited and were forcing the warehouse door when the bureau vehicles screeched to a stop. Roma and Burgis jumped out and converged, along with the other agents, on the building's entrance just as it was thrown open. And then everything went black.

There was a crash from inside the warehouse but Cameron couldn't make out what had happened. The lights had gone out within the building. As had the overhead cabin light in the auto he was seated in, while its dashboard had gone as dark as the tablet Roma had left behind.

He opened the door and got out. All the lights within and on all of the autos appeared to have been affected. One of the agents was running back to their vehicle. They reached inside and pulled out a flashlight which also failed to work. It was the same with their radios and phones.

Somewhere, Cameron suspected, the air-boys were watching and laughing.

People Like You

"When my old friend, Vishal, called me and told me that I needed to come to Delhi, immediately, I was unconvinced. To say the least.

"I had remained in Oxford and started a business. It was hardly setting the world alight but it paid the bills for me and my family so I was reluctant to drop everything and get on a plane; especially when he wouldn't even tell me what his new idea was. And then he said, 'Noel, it's not an idea. I've done it. All the things we used to talk about; all the plans we had to make things better. I've done it.' And he had.

"Now, fifteen years later, a blink of the eye in terms of human civilization, two thirds of the world's nations are powering their homes, shops and factories with C47 and an explosion of clean industrial innovation has thrust us into a new age. That's what Subah, the organization we built together, and our partner nations have achieved but I would like to take a moment to speak on what we have lost in that time too.

"We lost the large-scale despoiling of our planet. We lost the delusions of superiority of a global elite; because once we could power the dreams of everyone, the creativity and industry of all peoples was impossible to deny.

"And we lost the hold of the ascetics. The self-deniers, the Spartans who decry all progress and despise all who refuse to live as they do. We stripped them bare and revealed them to be the anti-development, anti-equality, anti-joy misanthropes they always were.

"On a personal note, I, to an extent, lost my friend; who decided the life of a celebrity scientist wasn't for him and stepped down as soon as we got our charter. He'll be on a beach somewhere with a drink in his hand. That's where he liked to be when he wasn't in the lab and, I'd say, he's earned his retirement. But, at some point he will catch up with the news so, on behalf of Vishal and myself, I accept this award and thank you from both of us."

Lawrence took a step back from the podium as the auditorium erupted. Most of the attending ambassadors got to their feet as they clapped. Most but not all, and, as if to show up the polite but brief applause of their fellows, the majority kept him standing to receive their approval while they made the great hall boom. Eventually, the General Secretary stepped up and led him off the stage. The applause continued behind them as the official guided Lawrence through a door where the noise merged with the clapping of a smaller assembly in a reception room.

Among the state and national officials were two grades of school children. The older group were the finalists of some science competition whereas the younger had been brought along from a local academy and didn't appear to know who Lawrence was beyond a white-haired old man and the center of all the attention. These little ones regarded him with such wonder he may as well have been a kindly wizard stepped from the pages of a storybook. He saw a more guarded version of the same in the eyes of the dignitaries as they came and went. The city's mayor stood beside him introducing them, one after the other, while Lonkar watched a few paces off.

"My son has a poster with a quotation of yours on his dorm wall."

"Really? What am I saying?"

"I don't remember," The mayor confessed. "Something inspiring." She continued before her tone changed. "By the way, I hope that nonsense this morning didn't cause too much distress? We're looking for the perpetrators now."

Lawrence smiled reassuringly. "My chaperone, Peter, here, was expecting worse. Young people will always make themselves heard. However misguided their beliefs may be they burn so fiercely at that age. We owe them our patience."

"It's wisdom like that we could all use, Mr. Lawrence. You know, his last birthday, I was looking for something for him, my eldest, and I realized you've never written about the early days with Vishal Vohra. No memoirs, no autobiographies, the best I could find were a book of interviews."

"I did have a life before all this, Madam Mayor."

"Of course, of course. I didn't mean…"

"But, certainly the last decade and a half has been exceptionally busy. If there is some small interest in my story, before and after the creation of the Subah Corporation, perhaps that's something I can address during my retirement."

The Mayor nodded and resumed her introductions until the General Secretary reappeared to escort Lawrence to yet another room to accept the award the United Nations had called him to New York to receive. He made another speech and stood smiling as a phalanx of photographers dazzled him. They would continue to snap away as he made a further round of handshaking and small talk, only ended when Lonkar informed him that they needed to set-off for the airport.

In the back of his auto, Noel Lawrence squinted through the sunroof and thought he could just make out the cradle of a window cleaner far above, as they drove through the city. The air-boys had been busy. In the early hours they had targeted the four highest towers in Manhattan and smeared them with an encircled triple 'T', the sign they had adopted for their impotent war-cry of 'tell the truth.' It had made the breakfast news but it would be forgotten before he was half-way across the Atlantic. They would be forgotten and Subah's mission would continue.

*   *   *   *   *

Horizon waited. As he had done for the last ten hours, upright on the middle board of the platform Imp and Miguel had built for him, twenty miles off the Atlantic coast and forty-three thousand feet in the air. They had christened this Frankenstein contraption the Roc; three air-boards bolted and strapped together with metal fastenings, their flight controls and spindizzies locked and working in unison.

It had taken him two hours to climb to this height and he needed to constantly correct and return to this spot when winds blew him from his holding position. He held it and he waited. It felt like he had been waiting for half of his life.

At least the weeks he had spent working with Polaris on his gear had already proved worthwhile. This high up normal lung function was impossible and the temperature around him read as minus fifty on his visor. Without a pressurized suit he would be unconscious in less than ten seconds and flash-frozen where he loitered. But, as things were, he was not only safe, he was invisible.

One of the things non-flyers could never grasp is why authorities had such a hard time tracking and stopping air-boys. They didn't understand that the very sophistication of the technology they used disadvantaged them because a radar system tuned to its maximum sensitivity would display nothing but a throbbing blob of undefined objects. Every large bird would show up on its screen. To be of any use, the systems needed to be filtered down to exclude anything too small, moving too slowly or, above a city, beneath a certain ceiling and for flyers like Horizon that left a lot of sky.

At this altitude things were different. He had lost count of how many fat airliners he had seen pass below him as he waited for one particular plane. The one carrying the man whose speech he had listened to while hovering above the clouds; the Subah corporate plasma-jet whose call-sign had just appeared on his visor's readout. It taxied to a runway and with minimal fuss was airborne. No one put

Noel Lawrence in a queue. The aircraft's code switched from red to green and was joined by altitude and speed readings. Climbing speed numbers beyond the dreams of an air-boy. It would already be a speck in the sky for those on the ground. He did not have long.

Horizon ran through a final checklist. He could feel the module in a pocket on his suit's leg but he tapped it anyway and reminded his fingers where the zip tab was. As he crouched to examine the bindings around his boots, the comforting weight on his back felt more reassuring than ever, though he was also aware of a stiffness that had crept into his limbs. That could not be helped. He trusted his body and, even as he occupied his mind cycling through the status readouts of the three boards he was about to push to their limit, he could feel his heart-rate increase and every sense he possessed sharpen.

Still crouching, he angled the Roc away from the approaching jet and watched its climb-rate slow on his visor as it neared its cruising altitude. When he turned his head back he could see it below him now, a metallic glint streaking above the sea, it was far smaller than an airliner but traveled much higher at forty thousand feet. Horizon looked forward again then tilted his body to reach his leading hand low enough to touch the Roc. It was the most he could do to minimize the drag of man and boards before flipping the rotors and switching from a hover to a powered dive.

The jolt was like nothing he'd felt before. Had it not been for the thinness of the atmosphere, all his mental preparation and careful positioning would have counted for nothing as the Roc combined with gravity punched him through terminal velocity, launching him downwards like an inverted moonshot. The Atlantic far, far below filled his entire field of vision. His visor display told him he was descending at mach 0.7 but the ocean remained serene and, to his eyes, fixed at a steady distance beneath him. It was an illusion he did not have time to ponder. Gently, Horizon began leveling out of his dive.

The maneuver brought increased stresses that told on the Roc immediately and the first red light began blinking on his visor. One of the rotors on the port air-board was close to burning out already. In ordinary flight he would simply slow down to preserve it but that was impossible here. It was an unwanted complication they had prepared for. Against Miguel's advice, he had instructed Imp to disable the safety protocols of all three spindizzies, meaning he could push them beyond their working tolerance envelopes. He kept the port rotor turning at full power.

At this speed he would be visible to Providence air traffic control. He would appear on their screens like a missile fired from nowhere. He would also have shown up on the Subah jet's radar by now but it was too late for them to do anything about that; its twenty meter length was already passing beneath him close enough to reach out and touch.

Horizon unzipped his pocket, retrieved the module and leaned down as more red lights began to flash in front of his eyes. He secured its magnetic base to the fuselage behind the fin-shaped antenna as the plane pulled away from him. These few seconds were the most he could keep up with a jet even had his own transport not been failing beneath him. As he ascended to avoid the plane's tail, the blast of its wake span him uncontrollably and he felt the Roc shatter.

The starboard air-board had broken free of its fixings and was falling in pieces into the Atlantic. The portside board was pumping out dark smoke, its rotors spinning at different rates, completely out of sync. Only the middle board seemed functional and there was no telling how long that would last. He was carrying a lot of extra weight.

He turned west, back to shore, and began as fast a descent as he thought he could safely manage. Even at this pace he should have disappeared again from radar screens. Unless someone had recalibrated their system to specifically look for him, he would remain a mysterious thirty second anomaly that had vanished as suddenly as it had blipped into existence. Soon he was level with the airliner corridors. The wash from one of these giants would have knocked him out of the sky but their flight paths were far behind him.

As he neared the coast, the faulty air-board's rotors spluttered and stopped completely. That was probably for the best as any additional lift it may have been providing came with the dangerous internal vibrations damaged boards were notorious for. Below him were rocks, then beaches, then streets with a patch of what looked like marshland beyond them. He bent low and uncoupled his boots, allowing the broken Roc to plummet to its final watery rest, and then spread out his body to slow his fall. At six thousand feet, he pulled the cord on his parachute and, a couple of minutes later, touched down in a field surrounded by woods.

There were some children chasing around a soccer ball who had stopped to watch him land. Horizon unscrewed and removed his helmet before calling one over.

"Is this South Kingstown?" The boy nodded. "Which way's the train station?"

* * * * *

The building the flyers had adopted for their base in New York was even larger than the riverside decoy. An old fulfillment center for an online retailer, it had an eight foot fence around it which made it more secure against most while making no difference to them.

The company that owned the building had assured the outer borough where it was located that a new hub they were seeking permission to construct next door would simply take on the current center's workforce. It never happened. Advances in robotics and plummeting power costs made it easier for them to automate the new site and transfer only a fraction of the workers. Since then, every proposal from prospective buyers to redevelop the old hub had been rejected while the retailer was still legally required to maintain and pay property taxes for the building. The security detail from the operating fulfillment center performed an hourly drive around the perimeter. It was a gesture, at best. The interior was so cavernous the flyers could be throwing a rave inside and no one would know.

At a couple of workbenches set up in a corner the group had divided into three. Fever, Polaris and Miguel occupied one bench with the flyers discussing torque-balancing while the latter bent over a laptop. At the other, Rayo and Imp, went through the photographs they had taken the night before. Imp's conclusions were sobering as he traced a finger across the surface of a tablet and zoomed in to better examine nocturnal rider and board both had observed from a rooftop across the river.

"It's a Corvette. Miguel agrees."

"I didn't know any were ever built." Rayo shook her head in disgust. "Is it armed?"

"I don't think so. You can see mountings but nothing attached to them. Even so, it's probably as fast as your Clipper." Imp moved his finger to the figure atop the air-board. "No idea what this backpack is. It could be power, I suppose. That would explain a lot."

"Do you know any batteries that size powerful enough to run an air-board the way he was riding it?"

"I do not. But Subah coming up with something new and keeping it in-house is easy enough to believe. If his board is C47-powered then they've already done that. Look at it; it's the darkest thing in the image, not one reflection. It has to be some new variant of the compound, hyper-efficient or capacitive, like we always suspected."

Rayo studied the photographs and was doubly thankful they had taken the time to lure in and ground this menace. They were no match for him in the air.

"Any word from Horizon?"

"No word but Gillian has been in touch. Another old flyer wants to pass on their board. Can you take care of it?"

"Sure."

Before they could discuss further, a triumphant bellow ended all conversation on the benches.

"He's done it! The module's live and transmitting." Fever, who was closest to Miguel, was soon at his shoulder watching data pour down the laptop's display. Polaris and the others joined him. "We now have access to every bit of information flowing into and out of that jet through its satellite up-link. Lawrence's log-in, the files he views, any additional passwords he uses while he's in the Subah system. Everything."

The group erupted into cheers and hugs. It was a moment they had worked towards since coming to the city. One they had all played their part in achieving.

Fever was first to think of their missing member. "I can't believe he pulled it off. That's some wild flying."

"I can believe it." Rayo answered. "Miguel, what's the flight time, New York to Delhi?"

"Fifteen hours. They've been in the air for about forty-five minutes now so minus that. Lots of time. The module's turned that entire jet into a packet analyzer. The data'll be encrypted but, we've got friends, they'll be able to break this."

As he replied, Rayo saw something among the cascading jumble of characters and leaned into the screen. It was an email address clearly legible within the chaos. Miguel followed her gaze and saw it too.

"That's just metadata. The content of whatever's in that mail is still encrypted. For now." He smiled up at her. "We won, Rayo."

She smiled back. It certainly felt like victory but with the feeling came the words she remembered Horizon using when he told her his plan. "Guys..." She called to the others and waited for them to turn to her.

"I've been doing a lot of thinking lately; and, the more I do, the surer I am, we are at the perceptible edge of history. This entire period is about to pass into books and recordings and lecture notes and those making them are happy to put us down as fools and leminos. Victims of our youth and underdeveloped judgment. That's their story. We know better.

"Someone once told me we were an 'unbroken chain.' From the Mirror Man, through Miguel, to us standing here; excepting that person, all the active flyers left on this continent. But if we fail in this mission, if we can't finally get the truth out of Subah, they'll be no one behind us. We are so few now, flyer culture will end and all we'll be remembered for is as their cautionary tale. We say 'no' and we continue to say it until the job is done and we have the proof of Subah's treachery in our hands.

"With strength, spirit and wisdom we will succeed."

* * * * *

"Are you sure you don't want to wait upstairs?"

Burgis recognized the tone and the nervousness behind the question. She had come down to Subah's New York office to see Peter Lonkar and then elected to remain downstairs in the building's lobby to await his return from the airport. Now the receptionist who she had informed of her decision was asking her to reaffirm it in order to forestall any impression of impoliteness or obstruction. Everyone had a boss and no one wanted them to receive unflattering reports of their conduct.

"I'm fine here." The receptionist returned to her desk and Burgis was left to her thoughts.

The operation to contain the flyers was over and she was satisfied with the outcome. They had not been able to prevent all incident but that, that there was amounted to little more than hooliganism which would hardly advance Horizon's cause. There had been no direct threat to Noel Lawrence's person and that was important. It eliminated the possibility of any heavy-handed response she would be required to spearhead.

The flyer community had maintained a campaign of harassment against the Subah Corporation for most of the last decade. It was mostly low-level stuff consisting of slander online and defacing local offices but they had snatched the odd briefcase and there was a Japanese air-boy still sitting in a prison in India two years after a foolish attempt to break into Subah's vast manufacturing facility and headquarters. Another casualty of the quest for the mythical archive.

What was she seeking when she chose to remain down here? Beyond indulging simple curiosity she wasn't sure. Lonkar had sequestered a floor of this small office block and she had spent many hours up there with him and his team. This liminal space she had passed through and barely acknowledged but this would be her last visit to Subah and the impulse to linger and see who else moved through it arrested her. It was plain, glass-fronted with bare walls in a neutral shade; a desk, some seating and, behind her, a bank of elevators. No senators, or CEOs, or mobsters, that she could recognize, walked by her as she sat there. The flow of smartly dressed men and women were as anonymous as those walking in and out of the buildings across the road.

Was this the aspect of Subah that so fixated the flyers, Burgis wondered. Everywhere yet unnoticed like the power cables and gas pipes it had made redundant but which still lingered beneath the city's streets. Her musings were cut short by Lonkar entering the lobby. She stood and offered her hand as he approached and they shook.

"Agent Burgis, I wasn't expecting you."

"I hope you don't mind me dropping by?"

"Not at all. Please," they walked on to the elevators together. "Are you well?"

"I am. It's always nice to complete an assignment and that's, kind of, why I'm here. I want to invite you and your team to a drink we'll be having tonight. Nothing raucous, just a small get-together at a bar downtown."

Lonkar nodded, thoughtfully, but perhaps for a little too long observed Burgis. "I won't say it's a Bureau tradition but... it's a Bureau tradition. And you can see the city, off the clock, before you fly home."

"I'm sorry, Agent Burgis, but I will not be able to attend tonight. I still have work to do."

"Noel Lawrence has left the country. The flyers have made their protest, injuring no one. Now they'll disperse."

"Did Gillian Tapp tell you that?"

"I'm sorry?"

"After our meeting you went back to her apartment, alone. I was surprised. This is not the sort of co-operation I was assured of by your government."

The elevator 'pinged' and rolled its doors open. Lonkar stepped into the cabin while Burgis chewed over his last statement. He reached out and prevented the doors closing between them. "Are you coming?" Burgis joined him in the cabin and they ascended.

"Ms Tapp was our only link to the air-boys. It seemed prudent, at least to me, to keep an eye on her. Following our encounter, last night, I revised that opinion."

"You mean the encounter that had your guy falling on his ass in the dark?"

"That EM pulse also wrote off two FBI vehicles. To return either to service you'd need to replace every electrical component in them. It's verging on terrorism."

"You let me worry about that." Burgis followed Lonkar out of the elevator to a security door which he swiped them through. "So, after placing an American citizen under surveillance without informing me, what did your revised opinion prompt you to do next?"

"Last night I retasked one of Subah's satellites. Since early this morning it has been in geo-synchronous orbit over the city. Filming everything." They had arrived at the closed door of a corner office. "I also made contact with some friends we have in Trondheim to make use of their facilities."

Lonkar opened the door to a dim interior, illuminated only by a wall-sized video projection of New York City viewed from above. The image had been processed to grey-out all the glare from C47 and, for reasons obscure to Burgis, would zoom into a particular rooftop or street corner for a closer look before expanding from that detail to its metropolitan overview.

Before the wall was a desk where two of Lonkar's team sat with their laptops. Burgis could observe variations of the wall image on their screens but they did not appear to be controlling the projected images' movements. She stepped inside the room.

"We established a downlink from the satellite to the Nidaros Enhet at nine:a.m. and it's been analyzing what we send it since then. If a flyer takes to the air, anywhere within the city limits, it will see them."

"How did you gain access to a quantum mainframe? They're supposed to be for research."

"We're paying them. Approximately one million dollars every thirty minutes."

Burgis was reeling inside. The implications of the words she was hearing, the words Lonkar spoke so casually, were so shocking they frightened her. Subah was out of control. They had developed as warped a view of the air-boys as the air-boys had of them. These two parties had been at war for so long; each could only see the worst in the other and attribute the darkest intentions to any and all actions. She turned to Lonkar. "Does the State Department know about this?"

"Apprehending the criminals you failed to prevent disrupting this visit is within the scope of your assignment, Agent Burgis. All I have done is mobilize Subah's resources to help you achieve that goal.

"Your naivety has been a hindrance I will no longer tolerate. These air-boys aren't kids with spray cans; they are a cell of anarchists and industrial saboteurs. And I will bring their threat to an end."

* * * * *

Miguel and the others had congregated around the laptop. They talked between themselves as he watched the data download itself onto the machine. The thought of all the doors it would open and all the secrets beyond those doors kept a smile on his face and, when he heard the faint sound of rotors, he assumed Imp had returned for something he had forgotten. Then Rayo was shouting and the desk, the laptop and all of them were being blown over. He hit the floor as the others scrambled away, scattering into the vastness of the building.

When he looked up, a flyer riding an air-board so black it seemed to suck in the light around it, was descending towards him. He hovered over Miguel. A full helmet obscured his face but the contempt in his voice was crystal clear.

"Was the EMP your idea, Imp?"

"My name's Miguel."

"I know who you are, Imp, and I can imagine how surprised you are to see me. They flew in my prototype overnight. It's not as fast or maneuverable as the board you destroyed yesterday but I think it'll do for your companions."

"Let's find out, hombre!"

Fever flew at the intruder so fast it was all he could do to dodge him and his swinging bat but he was ready for Polaris. As the air-boy approached, he raised his right arm and with it a cylindrical device attached to both his forearm and, through tubing running along the exterior of his suit, to a tank on his back. The device exploded twice and Polaris' air-board was hit, first at the fore of the board and then the underneath, as he veered away.

Rayo, who had been following him in, broke off her attack. She watched in disbelief along with Fever and Miguel as the air-board, now coated with two blasts of an ink-like substance, lost power and Polaris crashed to the floor.

"Call me, Sin." The night-flyer growled.

Miguel had seen enough. He got to his feet and waved his arms at his friends. "Go! Go now."

Rayo and Fever raced off, in different directions, while Sin turned to Miguel. "Where is Horizon?"

"Not here and you'll never find him." He began to make his way over to Polaris. Behind his back he heard Sin's rotors spin-up and carry him away.

* * * * *

Burgis stood before the image projected on the wall. The Enhet's analysis of the satellite's data-stream inserted a ten minute delay into the feed from Norway. It was this processing that had identified flyer activity and zoomed in on the structure the movement had originated from. The Subah technicians had switched over to a live feed, directly from the satellite, prior to their operative's arrival and entry through the roof. Now they watched two different flyers emerge and take diverging flight-paths.

"Where is he?" Lonkar demanded next to her.

"I don't know, sir, but we have a possible ID on one of the flyers. Call-sign: Fever, American air-boy in illegal possession of Subah technology. Never before seen in this city or state. We'll have to get closer to be sure."

Within her chest, Burgis' heart skipped a guilty beat at the mention of the name. Everyone else was too absorbed in events unfolding on-screen. Appearing through the roof and speeding from the building, Subah's operative set off in pursuit of the other flyer.

"Negative. Stay with Three-Zero."

* * * * *

Before the scheme to ground the night-flyer had taken shape, Rayo and the others had worked out a different plan. If he ever got the drop on a group of them, they would all take off in different directions and she, as the one with the fastest board, would dawdle to make herself the most enticing target prior to turning on the speed and leaving him in her wake. That had been the plan and Fever and she had followed it but it wasn't working. Her Clipper was maxed out but the tail she had successfully picked up remained with her. He wasn't making up the distance between them but he wasn't falling back either. This was a problem.

There was a tone in her earpiece followed by a voice, "Unknown flyer, respond." An unwelcome one. "Unknown flyer, I know you use this control channel.

We've heard your squawks to each other on it. Respond now."

He was broadcasting in the clear. If Rayo chose to reply, their comms systems would automatically shift their exchange to its own frequency and apply an encryption algorithm. But she had nothing to say to him.

"You're just putting off the inevitable. Look how low the sun is. It sets in ninety minutes. Even if you can stay ahead of me, what will you do then? We'll be in open country soon. By nightfall there won't be so much as an illuminated billboard to power that Clipper. And I won't lose a second.

"Stand down now and I'll only take the air-board. Keep this up and you'll lose your liberty as well."

It was not an idle threat. As she had departed their old base, she had seen a convoy of vehicles with flashing blue lights approaching it below her. Miguel and Polaris were likely already in custody. The latter in custody and, perhaps, worse as she had not seen him move once he'd hit the floor.

Rayo considered her options. None of them were good. If she could not out-pace Sin she would have to lose him and the small towns and townships they were currently racing over would be no use for that. There were other, larger conurbations further on but none offered the density and noise she needed. The interior of New York State was a flight path to nowhere for her.

Reluctantly, she adjusted her course to begin a slow arc that would take her back to the city. Her pursuer realized what she was doing and made a couple of attempts to cut

70

her off but all Rayo need do was arc out a little further and then reset her course for the metropolis. She saw him raise his arm once without firing his weapon. That was unfortunate. She was confident she had remained at a safe distance so a wasted shot would have given her an idea of its effective range.

Sin spoke up in her earpiece. "Don't say I didn't give you a chance."

Rayo looked back. He had made up a little air in her maneuvering but not much and could gain no more. His prototype while more powerful was also far bulkier than her Clipper. If she pushed on at full speed, he couldn't catch her while there was still light. Below them the green spaces diminished, roads converged and buildings grew higher. Soon the vertical peaks of Manhattan were rushing towards them and, from beneath and unseen by either, another figure rose to intercept.

At the last moment, Sin flipped his rotors and banked clear of Fever and his second swing at the Subah flyer. Fever looped high and made his feelings known through his comms, turning the control channel as blue as the darkening sky and alerting Rayo to his unexpected intervention. She slowed and swung around.

"What are you doing here?"

"I was listening in. The plan was a bust. That's why you turned back, right?" He fidgeted with the bat in his hands. "I can't believe he dodged me, Rayo. I was in a blindspot. He must have eyes on us. Other eyes."

Sin hovered a little way off. He was excluded from the conversation but he knew it was occurring. Together, the three mapped the points of a slowly rotating triangle nine hundred feet above the city. If they remained there too long they would be joined by NYPD drones sent to investigate.

"How is this a better plan? Now two of us are in danger instead of just one."

"No, still only one of us. You might be faster but I'm the better city-flyer. Let's see if he can keep up with me."

"He doesn't need to catch you to take you down, Fever."

"Yeah, I know. Get going. It's my party now."

Sin watched Rayo speed away and turned to Fever. "Very noble. But who's going to rescue you from me?"

"The way I see it, I won't need rescuing. All I have to do is out-fly you."

"It's Fever, isn't it?"

"My fame grows."

"Stand down now and I'll only..." Sin watched the air-boy drop, straight down, the grin on his face beaming up at him during a powered dive. "Have it your way."

Fever was descending into a mid-rise neighborhood of blocks with just enough variation in layout to offset it from a standard grid. He reversed his rotors as he fell past the paneled roofs and slowed to a stop, thirty feet above the sidewalk. He could see Sin, a black streak in the sky, following him down. Here, at this altitude and at the velocity he intended to push them to, his chaser's maximum speed would cease to be an advantage.

Slaloming through buildings, timing and control was everything; he did not intend to stay in a straight line long enough for Sin's board to make a difference.

As he was about to move off, he noticed an open window and a kid watching him. Yankees posters decorated the walls in the room behind the boy. Fever looked at the bat in his hand and then the boy and tossed the bat to him. His little hands reached out and caught the unexpected gift. When he looked up to thank his benefactor, Fever was already gone.

The rush was what he lived for. The wind on his face, the air-board beneath his feet, the smearing of the world around him and what came beyond that when he felt his heartbeat begin to slow and the blur retreated to the periphery of his vision; a multicolored abstraction, revealing an optical and dimensional clarity Fever knew no other way to access. The illusion of duality collapsed and his thoughts and body became one. At the speed he was racing through the city his life depended on it.

His turns were sudden and sharp, his path entirely random. The streets below him and the sky above dimly registered as elements around the now, the half a second from now and the one second. Fever had looked back twice. At first Sin was on his tail and then he wasn't. Before him New York had become a labyrinth with no beginning, end or meaning beyond his flight. It might have stayed that way if not for the sound of an impact almost immediately lost behind him.

He took another corner onto a wide avenue, turned and looked up. Chasing him, high above the rooftops, Sin followed. He raised his arm and Fever swerved to his right and banked left down an alleyway. The inky projectile slammed into the roof of an auto with a thunk.

"Coward! You're the night-flyer? You're the one I've heard about all these years? Too afraid to come down here and ride that board."

"Fear is irrelevant. You're dangerous. I'm here to stop you."

"Dangerous? You've forgotten what this is. Hovering up there like a drone trying to get a clean shot. I feel sorry for you." Fever said the words but his concern was mainly for himself. If Sin would not play his game he needed a different one; one that provided better cover than darting through side streets.

The sight of a stone tower glimpsed between blocks jogged his memory to a feature that might provide a temporary solution. Traveling high above the city these past weeks, he had observed a sliver of wooded parkland running next to a riverside highway and that antique water tower was one of its landmarks. The erratic course he had been flying, first to lose his pursuer and then to keep Sin from over-flying him, served him now but there was only so much more he could do to disguise his approach. As the tower loomed, Fever gunned his rotors and made a dash for the tree line.

He looked back and saw Sin descending raising his arm but, in an instant, he was crashing through branches and beneath the canopy. Sin flew straight over him and then doubled back before swinging off to the right. He couldn't see him. Fever kept his board powered-up but only enough to keep him above the forest floor with an accompanying hum too gentle to be heard more than a few feet away, let alone at Sin's altitude over the noise of traffic and people.

The trees comprising this urban forest were hardly mighty, yet they were numerous and their thin peeling trunks rose high and spread their branches wide. If he recalled correctly, they followed the highway which followed the course of a river for a couple of miles. It was an opportunity to, if not sneak clean away, at least, get a good head start on Sin. All he had to do was to exit these woods as far as possible away from his pursuer.

Gently, Fever edged forward over the uneven ground. Two months from now this forest floor would be dry and leaf-covered and, even floating as he was on minimal power, the displacement of dead foliage might give away his position. Today he remained invisible as a shadow passed, again, overhead. Sin was still searching but moving in the opposite direction from the one in which he was headed. He glided through the woods, occasionally ducking beneath a low branch and hoped his luck would hold out. In his favor, the setting sun washed everything but the long shadows he passed among the same dark amber. It was good camouflage.

He could still hear the highway but its rumble sounded further away than he knew it was. More present were the buzzing insects wheeling around him and birdsong. Sitting at the base of a tree, a pair of confused raccoons watched him drift by and, for a moment, he might have forgotten what he was doing there. The roar of rotors and smashing of branches, close behind, reminded him.

Sin had grown tired of scanning the woods from above and descended to flush out his quarry. The sight of birds taking to the air was an indicator worth investigating and his arrival beneath the canopy was immediately rewarded with a glimpse of the air-boy who had led him here. He pushed forward swiping down-hanging branches out of his way. The trees were a ragged chicane he forced as much as flew through straining for another sign of Fever. The air-boy had disappeared again.

Sin burst through the tree-tops and continued to rise. Above the nearby roofs and above the high-rise blocks up ahead while he scanned his surrounding. His visor's sensors searched streets and sky for a flyer's movement and came up with nothing. Yet movement there was. His own eyes caught the end of a wake as it settled into the river's soft lapping. He repositioned himself over the water and saw Fever, below the shoreline embankment and racing, perhaps a foot above the waterway's surface.

Fever had looked back twice. At first the sky behind him was clear and then it wasn't. Sin was bearing down on him at a pace he could barely believe. Either bank offered a return to the concrete maze of streets and avenues but it was already twilight and soon his air-board would begin to lose power. Attempting to escape this pursuer under such circumstances would be futile. He was running out of light, running out of cover and running out of tricks. It was time for something stupid.

There was a residential tower in his path looming over the far bank. Without allowing a moment to second guess himself, he swept across the river and reared up the glass and steel exterior of the building. The balconies of luxury apartments rushed by on either side of him until he saw what he was looking for and looped back on himself before hurtling through an open balcony door and reversing his rotors. He came to a stop in a lounge, over a dinning table and a family having their evening meal. The blast of his air-board's adjusting rotors scattered food and crockery everywhere as his astonished hosts fell away.

Fever spotted the apartment's front door and flew over to it. He did shout back an apology as he departed but it was unlikely anyone heard him over the screaming. In the hallway outside he picked a direction and turned on the speed, reaching a fire door and barging through it to the stairs. He had been hoping, unrealistically, for an open well he could descend through vertically. Instead he found a single incline of steps and a wall, around which would be the same. A sign told him he was on the fifteenth floor which meant thirty-plus sharp turns at speed. He set off.

Sin hovered a while outside the apartment. The occupants were picking themselves up, still dazed. He retreated into the gloam before they saw him.

Thirty-four sharp turns later, Fever entered the sub-level auto park. He didn't dismount until he reached the ramp up to street level and, cautiously, poked his head out. After a few seconds, Sin appeared. He was circling the building ensuring there could be no escape this time.

Fever took off his jacket and then his t-shirt, turned it inside out and put it back on before running a hand over the edge of the air-board, his air-board, hovering beside him. "Return to home." The board's rotors span-up and it raced off into the sky. Fever watched it go and a moment later saw Sin chasing after it, leaving the way clear. He removed his goggles and flight-com and stuffed them into his pockets then jogged up the ramp and fast-walked away from the tower.

It was a warm summer evening and along the riverside walkway, commuters on their way home and couples and groups on their way out, had stopped to watch the drama unfolding in the sky. Sin had caught up to the riderless board and hit it three times. He hovered above as it fell into the water and sank. Fever watched also, hidden among the gawkers on the embankment. He was one of them now. Soon there was another distraction; a quartet of police autos, lights flashing and sirens wailing, pulling up outside the apartment block. It was time to go.

Sin watched the officers pile out of their vehicles and enter the tower knowing they were already too late. He didn't really mind and his night wasn't over. He opened a secure channel to Subah. "Three-Zero Control, second stray neutralized. Send me the location of the first one."

"We have no location," the technician replied, sheepishly. "We lost them. So did the Enhet. We're not sure how, we're analyzing the..."

He dropped the line and switched his comms to broadcast in the clear to every flyer listening. "You can hide, little air-girl, you can hide for now. Sin will find you."

Sightlines

Gillian hurried down the sidewalk with her phone in her hand. She was in such a hurry her eyes had scanned and already dismissed the entrance to a side street before a voice called her name. A hooded Rayo emerged from the shadows of the unlit alleyway and nodded to her.

Gillian raised the phone. "Brendan, I've found her. Keep on going and you'll see me. There's enough room for you to back in." And then put it in dark-mode.

"Is he GC?"

"No, but he's a good friend. I trust him. What happened?"

"The night-flyer happened."

"I thought you'd grounded him?"

"So did we."

"What about the hack? Is it still transmitting?"

"It's over. Miguel has a drive-scrambler on his laptop. As long as he had time to activate it, they won't know what we were trying to do. At least until they find our scanner on the jet.

"That plan is done."

Rayo took out her own phone and crouched by the curb. Placing a hand at each end of the device, she pressed it into the corner of the step until it first bent and then snapped. Gillian watched her carry the phone's remains to a dumpster and dispose of them within.

"I was doing some research on it."

"Didn't you use a mask?"

"I did. But we're not taking anymore chances." The alley was lit up by a pair of red braking lights and they stood to the side. "We'll talk more when we get to where we're going."

Gillian made the briefest of introductions while Rayo loaded her air-board into Brendan's auto. She sat in the back when they got underway with her arm on a picnic blanket covering her Clipper. Up front, Gillian and Brendan talked; about work, about traffic and about houseplants Brendan didn't have but Gillian thought would look nice in his place. Gillian kept the chatter going and neither mentioned the young woman sitting behind them in possession of a notifiable piece of technology.

It had been a long day. An early start decorating skyscrapers in Manhattan followed by a nervous wait for confirmation of Horizon's success, the celebration of which was abruptly, violently, cut short. From there things had continued to go wrong and Rayo realized now she was exhausted. She drifted off on the way out to the suburbs and only came to her senses as they were pulling into a garage at Brendan's house. He looked up at her in the rearview once they stopped. It was a friendly face with soft, portly features and an open smile.

"Welcome to my place. You can stretch your legs here with Gillian. I'm going to go upstairs and make sure the air-con is working in your room."

Gillian raised an eyebrow at Rayo. "New Yorkers think this is hot." She waited until they were out of the auto and alone before continuing. "There was some news on the radio while you were asleep."

"What was it?"

"The reports are confused. An air-board and a rider or just an air-board, fell into the Harlem River a little while back. The eyewitnesses can't agree on what went into the water but they all say there was another flyer there at the time."

"He calls himself 'Sin.' I don't know if it's boast or confession." Rayo looked around the garage. There was no way she was going to stow her board here. She would carry it up to the room her host was preparing for her. "Did anyone come out of the water?"

"Not that anybody spotted. This is a disaster, Rayo. How did you get away?"

"Fever was convinced they had an overwatch position so…"

"Sorry, what?"

"It wasn't just the night-flyer. Someone was monitoring us and helping him. I flew under some elevated rail tracks and followed them for a while. Then, at a junction, I saw a garbage truck approaching. I waited and dropped into the back and hid beneath the claw-arms."

"You did what?" Gillian demanded before remembering herself and lowering her voice. "Those things are compactors. You could have been crushed to death."

"It was the only way. There's an overhang at the rear so I could get in with my board and not be seen. I was only in there for a half a dozen blocks. I jumped out at a set of lights."

"No, no, no. This is too much…" Gillian had her hands on her head and had begun pacing the garage. "We have to end this before someone gets killed."

"Fever might be dead already. We don't know."

"He's not dead. He's too good a flyer."

"He's not a flyer at all anymore. Subah took him and Polaris down tonight and Miguel's probably sitting in a police cell right now. We're not ending anything, Gillian, and I need some information from you."

Gillian stopped pacing and did her best to compose herself.

"How many active flyers are there left in Europe?"

"A handful. It's just like here. Scattered, barely connected."

"Are there any left in France?"

"Only one I know of. His call-sign is 'Greenray.' He flies out of Paris. Why do you want to know about European flyers?" Rayo was silent. "Are you going to Europe?"

"Please stop. Gillian, there was a reason I asked you to find me somewhere to stay outside of the ground crew network." She paused and considered her next words, searching for the least painful way to proceed. "They'll be needed here to support Polaris and Miguel. We don't want them to have any connection to what happens next, in case it goes wrong."

"What is happening next?"

"I can't tell you. And I need your flight-com." Rayo held out her hand. "If they weren't following you before, they will be now. You shouldn't be caught with it on you."

"What if you need me again?"

"We won't."

"You won't? Have you discussed this with Horizon?"

"Horizon, Imp and myself all agree this is the right thing to do. You're not a flyer, Gillian. You never were. You shouldn't have it anyway."

Gillian looked at Rayo's open hand. Eleven years she had been chronicling flyer society and now the flyers were rejecting her. Just like that. She reached into the auto and took out her bag, carrying it over to Rayo, before dropping the flight-com's earpiece and matchbox-sized transceiver into the waiting palm. These weren't the air-boys she knew.

"It's for the best. With Lawrence gone, things will quieten down."

There was nothing more to be said so Gillian made no reply. She left the garage and walked down Brendan's driveway to the street.

*   *   *   *   *

Miguel had caught a glimpse of the exterior from the police transport. The lights at its base couldn't reach its summit which was a solid black against the night sky but, at ground level, the building's very mass and grayness seemed designed to intimidate and drain hope from arriving inmates. He kept his head up as he was walked past the barred doors to row after row of dormitories and, to his surprise, found himself deposited in an empty cell.

Two hours later he was escorted to a small interview room where a woman was waiting for him. She was seated and looking at her phone as he entered. When she saw him she slotted it into an inside pocket of her jacket.

"Miguel Pinto, my name is Mia Burgis. I'm a special agent with the FBI."

"I already spoke to you people."

"You didn't say much."

"No I didn't and I don't intend to now. My lawyer will be here in the morning. I can ignore all of your questions, more formally, then."

"The morning is hours away. Don't you want to know what happened to your friends?" She gestured to the chair across the table from her.

"And what do you want?"

"We can get to that."

Miguel walked over and sat down. "Polaris?"

"You know it would be easier to get in touch with his family if we had his real name?"

"His family is who that psycho in black you sent chased off."

"I didn't send him. Subah sent him. And they think they know who you are; an O.G. flyer from New York City, call-sign, Imp. Is it true?"

He was already running out of patience. "Tell me about Polaris or we can wrap this up right now."

"Two broken ankles, three broken ribs." Burgis watched Miguel's face darken. "But the doctors tell me he's young and fit so he'll recover fully. It'll just be a painful, slow recovery." The phone began to buzz in her pocket. She took it out, rejected the call and put it away again.

"And the others?" He asked quietly.

"The other two got away. One of them, Fever, I believe he calls himself, had to sacrifice his air-board to do it but we don't know where he is."

"So then he didn't get away."

Once again she was struck by the oddness of this group. Try as she might, Burgis couldn't see this culture as anything other than deeply unhealthy or understand the hold it had on people like the man before her. She watched him process the information she had just imparted, assessing injuries and calculating futures, as he fought his way to a stoic acceptance of where he was right now and how little he could do to effect things. This was where she wanted him.

"You didn't come down here just to tell me all this, Agent Burgis. If you got some kind of deal to offer me, you're wasting your time."

"Deal? Mr. Pinto you were discovered in illegally occupied premises with known and suspected law-breakers and your prints are all over the laptop we found. Our people are working on that now, by the way. No, your goose is cooked and I am entirely comfortable with that outcome."

"Then why are you here?"

"That's a good question. I'm here because when I talk to flyers and their allies about Subah, all I hear is, to be blunt; paranoia, misdirected anger and boogie-man reasoning. This from people who otherwise seem intelligent and, reasonably, well-adjusted.

"So, as a law enforcement professional I have to ask myself, is that all it is? Or is there anything more? Any solid evidence on which they base their wild ideas about the corporation."

Miguel sat back in his chair watching Burgis. For the first time since entering the interview room he wasn't sure what to make of her. "Can I see some ID?"

She took out her badge and card and lay their leather holder open on the table between them. He looked them over carefully before raising his eyes to her once again.

85

"The air-boys weren't stupid. After The Fall various people looked up the line of dealers, smugglers, paid-off officials. Dust isn't like a narcotic, you can't cut it with ground glass, it reads different. The line stretched all the way back to Subah."

Burgis shook her head. "Anecdotal."

"What do you expect? You want ledgers and invoices? After all the deaths, the supply-line collapsed but, while it was there, it went back to Subah's facility in India. Nothing had changed. Nothing had changed but the dust."

In her jacket, Burgis' phone began to vibrate again. "Give me a second." This time she took it out and answered to a flustered Roma.

"Lonkar has been here, cooling his heels, for half an hour. He says you were supposed to meet him."

"Tell him I was unavoidably delayed and I'll be there in ten. Get him a cup of coffee."

"Seriously?"

She terminated the call. "Mr. Pinto, thank you for meeting me. I'm sure your lawyer can keep you updated on the condition of your friend from now on."

"That's it?" Miguel asked. "Am I going to see you again?"

"Not unless it's in court."

She had not been expecting much yet Burgis was still disappointed. Her first sit-down with an actual air-boy and all he could give her was more flyer lore. She could do nothing with this.

A guard conducted her back to the entrance where she handed in her visitor's badge and exited to the clanking of heavy doors and buzzers. Beside her auto she took a moment to take in the detention center. It was like a fortress. Then climbed inside and pulled down her seatbelt. "Federal Plaza." The auto started up and moved off.

Earlier that evening, from Subah's control room, she had called Roma and told him to cancel the team drinks. He had been more intrigued than upset and eager to hear what new developments had postponed their celebration. The scope of Subah's covert action was not something she was willing to share on the phone, however, and her growing unease with their partners she would save for her report.

To his credit, Lonkar remained calm when he saw her, though she believed it took some effort. He rose to his feet slowly with the air of a man fighting himself rather than gravity as he informed her that he had been waiting there an hour. As she pulled out her chair, Roma, at the next desk, stared even harder at the papers before him.

"Unavoidably detained. I'm sorry I kept you waiting."

"You're not going to tell me where you were?"

"No. No I'm not." Burgis sat down. "Have you updated my colleague?"

"Yes. Although I believe certain operational details are best omitted from the record for now. I trust you'll agree with my choices."

"I'm sure I will."

"And a recovery team has been booked for tomorrow morning. I'll be there myself to take custody of the stolen technology as soon as it's brought up."

"Excellent. Sounds like you didn't need me after all."

"If only it were so," Lonkar sighed. "My people have lost sight of Gillian Tapp and I don't think it is a coincidence it happened on this night. I need you to find her and bring her in."

"You mean arrest her?"

"If need be."

"Well, that's a problem because I have no grounds on which to do that. You never cleared your surveillance of her with me so you were, effectively, operating as a private agency. I'm not going to jump in now unless I've got good reason."

Lonkar bristled. "I'm sorry?"

"This is America. We don't just arrest people for the hell of it." Burgis turned to Roma who had been listening to the exchange with mounting concern. "Have you tried calling her?"

"Voicemail. The phone's dark. We'd need to upgrade her from 'associate' to 'suspect' for active discovery measures and you have to sign-off on that."

Burgis looked up at Lonkar. "Well, I'm not going to."

"Agent Burgis, we spoke earlier about co-operation, do you remember?"

"I do."

"This is an example of an occasion when I would expect it. There is no order of moves here and we cannot simply wait; to do that is to allow our adversary time to regroup and strike back. We have the advantage. We must press and continue to press until we break them.

"Gillian Tapp is surely part of this cell's support system. We must increase the pressure on it by denying them her aid. This is what I and the Subah Corporation require from you right now."

Burgis had been waiting all evening to say this, "Mr. Lonkar, I do not work for the Subah Corporation." And it felt good. "I thank you for your assistance in locating the flyer base and securing the suspects we have in custody. If further investigation links Gillian Tapp to them, she'll be rolled into that case but the Bureau will be doing the investigating and doing it within the law, not you.

"Special Agent Roma, can you see our guest out."

Lonkar's face before he stormed off was at least one pleasant memory Burgis could take from this day. Roma had to hustle to catch up with him as he strode from the office. Her young colleague returned ten minutes later and stood before her desk.

"I'm not going to pretend I know what's going on, boss, but that didn't seem smart."

"Did he say anything as he was leaving?" Roma shook his head. "It's late, go home."

"What about you?"

"I'm going to make a start on my report."

"I thought we weren't done with this assignment?"

"It's gonna be a long report. Go home, Ted."

When she was alone, Burgis started going through the case file at her desk and was immediately confronted with a name that gave her pause. Cameron Herrick had good grades and a bright future. With a broadcast engineer and a teacher for parents, he could hardly be any more suburban and unremarkable. She had gone in a little harder on him than she had needed to. She regretted that now.

Burgis closed the file and took it up along with a Bureau tablet and her phone and swung out from her desk. She had a lot of reading ahead of her and she wanted do it somewhere a little more comfortable. There was a breakroom on this floor she had never spent much time in but, right now, its easy chairs, water cooler and even the trio of potted plastic spider-plants seemed the very oasis she required. The hum of air conditioning and routers faded into silence as she left the office.

In the breakroom she found a chair to recline in and opened the file on her lap. Two months ago the United Nations announced that they were going to hold a reception for Noel Lawrence to mark his retirement and, almost immediately, the FBI began picking up whispers the local air-boys were mobilizing. She had been told to pick a small team to start gathering intelligence on Horizon and determine his intentions. A hardcopy of the letter officially commissioning the assignment and appointing her as lead agent was the first page in the file.

Her lids became heavy rereading the letter. The recollection of all the dead ends she had encountered trying to infiltrate the flyer community made it seem like longer ago than it was. It had been the first sign this job wouldn't be the high-profile, low-risk gig she had initially taken it to be. She turned the page and continued reading and then turned another and another again before realizing that her phone, resting on the chair alongside her, was ringing and there was a funny taste in her mouth. She reached out and answered the incoming call.

"Boss? Where are you?"

It was Roma. "Didn't I tell you to go home?"

"I did go home. Last night. I'm in the office now and your jacket is still over your chair."

Burgis looked down to see that half the papers from the case file, still balanced on her lap, were now on the floor. She examined her phone's screen for the time and groaned. She had spent the night in the breakroom.

"Are you okay?"

"I'm fine." There was a stiffness in her back that betrayed her words but she kept that to herself. "Anything new?"

"One thing. Gillian Tapp's phone's reconnected to the network. We've got a location for her. It's not what I was expecting."

"I'll be right there."

*   *   *   *   *

The divers located the spoiled air-board quickly and brought it to the surface. Lonkar had insisted on joining them on their launch and taking possession of the dangerous apparatus right there on deck. He zipped it into a large, light and radio-proof bag and conveyed it to Subah's New York base where it could be secured while he returned to the satellite monitoring room.

The captured flyer, Polaris, had been given a bed in a tenth floor private suite of a city hospital. Lonkar sat in the darkened room watching a live feed of the building while the Enhet tracked every moving thing within the metropolis. A couple of blocks away from the hospital, Sin surveyed the sky from the vantage point of a half-completed tower, its scaffolding and sheeting shielding him from view. He could see Polaris through the windows of his suite.

Their quarry had gone to ground since they had lost track of the first flyer the night before and Lonkar was concerned. This trap was a long shot but air-boys were irrational. He may no longer be able to rely on the FBI but the warped idealism of flyer culture persisted and the cost did not concern him. The expense of hiring the Enhet would be split between one hundred and thirty nations. Subah's subscribers would pay a little more next year and no one would question it. People rarely questioned Subah.

So they would wait and watch.

*   *   *   *   *

Brendan knew the shift patterns for both Gillian and himself so he noticed when she did not turn up for work. He had kept an eye out for her strolling in, as she usually did, five minutes before she was due on the shop floor but she never showed up. Finally, he asked one of the managers about her and was told that she had called in sick.

At lunch he had given her a call and then again during his afternoon break but both times her phone rang without answer. He began to worry, only a little and only because he did not believe that she was really sick, as she had been fine last night. He expected she was off on some mission for her friends, perhaps the one currently lodging in his parents' old room.

In the years that he had known Gillian, she had never gone into detail about her ongoing association with these flyers and he had never wanted to press her. It seemed something between a hobby and a second job which he could understand she might need as the one they shared at the store was hardly the most stimulating.

Brendan pondered Gillian's silence on his drive home whereupon his musings were finally put aside while, pulling into his garage, by the unexpected aroma of home cooking. It welcomed him back like a warm hug. He had experienced nothing like this since his mother had passed away yet these scents were different. On entering the house, he discovered that Rayo had been to the market and returned with fresh ingredients to prepare them a feast. It was her way of saying thank you.

During the meal, he told her about the only other time he had seen a real air-board, in a design museum in Manhattan. He had been lucky because although the exhibition had been slated to run for two months, Subah had confiscated the item barely a week into the show. To Brendan's surprise, Rayo was aware of the incident though she could not have been more than eleven or twelve when it occurred. She described the look of the board exactly as he remembered it and even knew the name of the flyer who had donated only to lose it.

As they drank coffee, Rayo asked for his aid once more. She and her air-board needed a lift but she would wait until they were in his auto and on the road before she told him where they were going. They drove for an hour and arrived, after nightfall, at an out of the way marina where a man in some kind of uniform met them at the gate.

His passenger leaned in and planted a kiss on his cheek before decamping and retrieving her board, still under a blanket, from the rear of his auto. She followed the man into the marina and Brendan watched them descend to a pier where a small boat was moored. Within the vessel was another figure who jumped to their feet when they saw Rayo. The two embraced before the uniformed man cast off and powered them out onto the ocean where Brendan could see the lights of a much larger craft waiting off-shore.

This had been a strange interlude. Even so he had been happy to help. His departing visitor had insisted he leave his phone at home but, when he got in, he would try Gillian again.

* * * * *

The fence was higher than Gillian remembered. Standing before it she guessed at eight feet and contiguous with another foot of barbed wire in three spiky rows. This she had come prepared for, the runner mat she had 'borrowed' from her parents' home hung over her shoulder, its heavy folds picking up the warm desert breeze blowing through the edge of Metro Phoenix.

She paced backwards a short stretch and then ran at the fence, leaping onto and securing a firm handhold while her toes sought support in the hexagonal mesh through her sneakers. She had been concerned about attempting this in the twilight but that had been a wasted worry. This was all feel. At the top of the fence, she dragged the long mat off her shoulder and laid it, doubled-over, across the barbed wire. Its fearsome thorns were reduced to pinpricks on her hands and knees as she traversed this final barrier. On the other side, Gillian hit the ground, rolled and then stood and dusted herself off.

Arizona and Southern California had been home to aircraft storage and salvage facilities for over a century. The wide open spaces and dry air made it ideal. This boneyard had existed on the outskirts of her hometown long before she had been born. It was much smaller back then and it had grown since her last visit. Gillian walked between the airliners, their windows catching the last of the red in a somber blue sky, and wondered whether there was anything so silent and still as a machine meant to thunder and soar. They had them lined up in neat rows like autos in municipal parking bays but this was a cemetery.

Most of the world's passenger planes ran on battery powered plasma-jets. The wide-bodied long-haul fleet, that needed more power, received it from C47 panels built into their wings. Subah controlled the whole process; their panels, their installation teams and aircraft built to the output and tolerance specifications they set. The planes she moved between now had once been the pinnacle of civil aeronautical engineering. Even when their technology evolved they had been an essential store for component and material spare parts. Now they were redundant. Stood down forever like her.

Gillian searched between the grounded giants looking for the spot where they had sat the last time she was here. The scale change made it difficult. The yard, as it was now, did not conform to her memories but she knew she was close. She recognized some of these dead machines and the sadness of the unfulfilled futures that haunted them. It hung about them visible even to her dusk-accustomed eyes. Eyes suddenly blinded. She raised a hand but the glare was all around her. It was coming from above.

For a second she thought about running. There were plenty of places to hide. The sound of an auto approaching dashed that idea. As it rolled to a stop before her, the drone, overhead, dimmed its spotlight. Gillian waited while the auto's two occupants disembarked and walked towards her. One face was familiar, the other not and neither were welcome.

"Special Agent Burgis, what a surprise meeting you out here."

"I could say the same. This is Special Agent Theodore Roma and we were both wondering what you're looking for?"

"Who says I'm looking for anything? Maybe I was out for a walk, I saw this place…"

"No, no, no…" Burgis was in no mood for games. "Keep that up and you'll be spending the night in a Phoenix police cell.

"Your little friends have gone quiet back East. Dropped off the map. You went dark too and then you show up here. What were you looking for in this place? Is it something for them?" Burgis watched a humorless grin spread across Gillian's face. "What's happened?"

"They don't want my help. They've made that very clear. And I don't know what they're planning so, if you've come to me for information, you're out of luck. What I do know is that it was you who made them outlaws."

"They were outlaws from their inception. They build those dumb boards with stolen tech."

"Industrial refuse."

"It doesn't matter. It was someone else's property. Now, once again, why are you here?"

Gillian looked past the agents and then around the boneyard, one final time, attempting to locate the spot she had been seeking. She had been arguing with people like Burgis for so long that it had become a habit, one that served her no longer when she was here to say goodbye.

"I was here with Brink. It was the last time I saw him. He had come down from California and he knew about this place so I brought him down here."

"So, you've broken in here before?" Burgis asked.

"We didn't break in anywhere. I stood on his board and he lifted us over the fence. It was a day like this. We sat and talked and night fell. I was trying to find where, exactly. Wasn't expecting the FBI to show up."

"Well, we did and now you're under arrest."

"Excuse me?"

"No. No, I won't," Burgis snapped. "Not again. What is wrong with you people? You think you can go anywhere, whenever you feel like it. You think you can turn peoples' lives upside down and run your shadow-ops with no consequence but that's not the world; there are rules in this world and I'm sick of all of you trampling over them like they don't apply to you." She turned to Roma "Put her in the back."

Roma took Gillian by the arm, walked her over to the auto and secured her in the rear before recalling the drone and storing it in the trunk. When he returned, Burgis had not moved. She was standing where he had left her, looking up at the sky.

"You okay, boss?"

"Do you believe her? All this, laying the memory of an old boyfriend to rest, stuff."

Roma shrugged. "They're Romantics. It fits their profile."

"Maybe." She was spellbound. It was the same night sky as the one over New York City but there was so much more of it. "Let's go home." Burgis said, finally, but remained where she was.

Harm Done

Imp silently congratulated himself for remembering to pack some sunglasses. His smart-goggles had glare compensation inbuilt but he didn't want to get them out even though he was sure the crew knew what he and Rayo were. An air-board is not an easy thing to hide so the effort his fellow flyer and he had made during this past week was an expression of politeness. If they were ever questioned, they could claim a guilt-free ignorance of their two passengers that worked for everybody.

The captain of the Cygnet, the yacht whose sun deck he currently lounged upon, had told him this was a thirty-five meter craft. Imp had spent much of the first two nights on the bridge talking to the crew. Though he was from a coastal city, the only time he spent on water was during ferry trips between the boroughs of New York, and he found the constant motion unsettling. At first they had taken him to be just a nervous traveler but when they realized that he had a genuine interest in machines, the first mate took him down below and showed him around. It had been years since he had seen a working internal combustion engine. And he had never seen one of the yacht's size.

The debate over whether to abandon fossil fuels had roiled the country during his early teens. The new compound had already been enthusiastically adopted in poorer states but many of the wealthier nations resisted. Every night on TV, senators would argue with union leaders, economists with defense analysts; schools were instructed to avoid the issue entirely while an emboldened environmental lobby began referring to petroleum as 'death juice.' It went on for years and then suddenly it was over and it seemed like C47 was everywhere.

"Nothing on the radio."

Rayo had managed to sneak up on him. She was barefoot and wearing a dress. It was a very different look from the one she had in the city. A city far behind them.

"We'll find out soon enough. The captain says we'll be in Southampton tonight."

"It could be a very short stay."

Rayo sat on the lounger beside Imp. "Have faith."

"That's about all we have left. Our home advantage is a thousand miles away. No ground crew to back us up. No Gillian and, if anyone saw us now, no reputation to speak of either."

"They made things too dangerous for our friends. Their enemies were the only ones we could rely on. And, once we get off this boat, it's flyers only until this thing is done." She sighed. "Perhaps that's how it always should have been."

Imp knew what Rayo was thinking. He had contemplated the cost of their mission and how little they, as yet, had to show for it. This final, desperate plan, cobbled together on a three-way flight-com exchange, was the last roll of the dice for them and the need for radio silence, once it had been put into action, meant his companion and he had no idea whether it had already fallen apart. The benefactors whose yacht they now occupied had earlier flown Horizon to Europe. They asked very few questions. They hated Noel Lawrence and Subah and that was reason enough to help.

"If I remember right, there are only two active flyers left in the U.K. but one of them is an Imp so I should be able to get a decent conversation, at least."

Rayo smiled and lay back on the lounger. "Whatever you say, New York Imp."

"Really?"

"Yankee Imp?"

"That's even worse."

"Gran Manzana Imp?"

"Please stop…"

*   *   *   *   *

Burgis opened the door to the meeting room to find one mystery explain another. She had been sent here by her immediate superior with no indication as to why they would not simply convene in his office. Sitting at the long table in the meeting room was, Thomas Eason, her first Section Chief on her first Bureau posting and the closest thing she had ever had to a mentor. He was a Deputy Assistant Director now and based in Quantico, so what brought him to New York was her first question after a hug.

"I came to see you, Mia. I asked to conduct this debrief." He nodded down to a hardcopy of her report. Directly across the conference table was an envelope before another chair. "Take a seat."

"Okay." Burgis noted his tone and, on seating herself, that the envelope in front of her had her name on it. "What's this, Tom?"

"We'll come to that." He leafed through the pages before him. "You went to see Miguel Pinto, alone, in the MDC; can you tell me why you did that Special Agent Burgis?"

"I was hoping an informal one-on-one might encourage him to open up."

"But it didn't. You got no new information pertinent to his case or helpful in apprehending the flyers still at large?"

"I did not."

"And you made no recording of the meeting?"

"As I said, I was trying to keep things informal. These people, all of them, they have a deep mistrust of law enforcement. Trying to connect to them as an individual rather than treating them as a suspect can, sometimes, pay off." As she spoke, he kept his eyes on his notes. Her mentor. Her friend. "As I believe you know, sir."

Eason looked up. "You did the same thing with Gillian Tapp, who you also failed to make an official suspect; something that may have enabled us to find her quicker."

Now Burgis knew where this was all coming from. It was Lonkar's revenge for not asking 'how high' when he had told her to jump. He had probably singed the ear-hairs of some fat senator who'd extracted a promise from the Bureau that she would be given a telling off. She straightened her back in her chair and prepared herself to accept the admonition.

"Sir, I accept that Subah security and myself differed in our assessment of the threat this group posed, but my focus never strayed from the objectives of my assignment: gathering intelligence on this criminal subculture and keeping Noel Lawrence safe.

"Lawrence departed without a flyer getting within shouting distance of him and they are two members down. Their protest scrawl was visible for a few hours. They lost, badly."

Eason nodded and drew in a long breath through flaring nostrils. He looked at her with an expression she couldn't quite pin down.

"Are you aware of the burglary that took place in Paris two nights ago, Special Agent Burgis?"

Burgis nodded. She had read of the incident. The details of what was taken and from whom had been withheld but local police suspected the robbers had entered the building, a large office block, through the roof.

"Subah have contacted the Bureau to tell us they believe one of the participants in that burglary was the air-boy, Horizon. Someone who we had in this city for a number of weeks and failed to apprehend."

"What was stolen?"

"We don't know but our sources, on the ground, tell us that Noel Lawrence's niece works in the office that was raided.

"Subah Security declined to confirm or deny that. In fact they're not really talking to us at all. They did, however, make it clear before they terminated contact that they believe you got too close to the air-boys and that your judgment has been compromised."

"What?"

"Why didn't you find and bring in Gillian Tapp when you were asked?"

"She hadn't done anything."

"Twenty-four hours later you arrested her for breaking and entering. Has it occurred to you that, had you been a little more pro-active, this crime may not have occurred?"

"With respect, sir, I don't think even the FBI is ready for anti-causal law enforcement."

Eason slammed an open palm on the table. "You think this is a joke?" His eyes were furious. "This was an assignment where you could have made friends, Mia, instead of which, you've done the opposite."

He took a moment to calm himself and turned over another loose page. Across the table, Burgis was starting to worry where this was all heading.

"Tom, I…"

"Open the envelope in front of you."

Burgis did as she was told and extracted a two-page job specification and a letter notifying her of her new posting. She scanned all three pages with growing astonishment. "This can't be right. This isn't a reassignment. It's a transfer to an entirely different division."

"Facilities and Logistics, that's correct."

"What am I going to do in Maine? Count moose?"

"You'll be the Deputy Fleet Manager for the whole of the state and based out there in the branch office. It's an important role. Autos need to be maintained, especially somewhere so rural."

"Sir, I don't believe I can accept this transfer." She let go of the pages and let them settle before her. She did not want to touch them. "And I am prepared to make formal representations to protest it. In my opinion, most reasonable people would recognize this as a punitive measure against me. One I do not believe I deserve."

Eason's voice was calm. "Look again at the grade, Special Agent." Wholly untroubled by the gauntlet she had just thrown down between them. "Technically, that role is a promotion; it's even a little more money than what you're on now. I'm not sure any tribunal will see it as punishment."

"Looking after autos? I'm an investigator not a mechanic. This is not what I was trained for."

"Special Agent Burgis, you were trained to serve the FBI in whatever capacity it required of you. And now it needs you in Maine. You would be unwise to refuse this reassignment but, of course, it is your choice."

The words seemed to echo around her head. What kind of choice was this? To accept a promotion downwards or that her time in the Bureau would end at the next apposite opportunity her superiors observed. Burgis had no doubt that is what she was being told without it being said. All her work, all the long hours, the study and discipline to get her to where she was; was it really to end on a procedural disagreement with an outside security department. It seemed absurd and yet here she was, unless, there was a third way. She cleared her throat.

"Sir, might not all this… administrative perturbance be avoided with a few clarifications, on my part, in the original report?"

Eason put down his pen, shuffled the loose pages before him into their folder and closed it. "We don't ask our people to rewrite reports, Special Agent. Can of worms."

He rose and came around the table to take the chair next to Burgis. "You haven't been abandoned." He said, quietly. "I remember, and I'm not the only one that does, that bright young prospect I first met years ago. I even recall thinking to myself, 'this one's going places.' But you need to regain your perspective. Take the reassignment."

"If I did…" She could hardly believe she was considering this. "How long would I be up there?"

"You bought a place in the city, didn't you?" Burgis nodded. "I'd be looking to let it out for eighteen months, at least. Maybe two years. Over the course of a career, that's nothing.

"Mia, take the reassignment."

* * * * *

Horizon made one final pass through the valley. Neither his eyes nor the enhanced optics of his smart-goggles could spot anyone, though he knew Rayo was down there hiding because they had set their flight-coms to automatically connect when they were in range. It was the only signal registering on his goggles' display.

This valley, sunk into the southern edge-lands between England and Wales, was so deep and its character so beautiful, no towers or booster stations had ever been built to fill in the information-stream dead zone its geography created. The lone structure here was a stone and slate house Horizon had passed twice over already and the only other person visible, the figure in black waiting outside who watched him now as he descended.

Horizon dismounted and stood back, "Loiter. Fifty feet." The air-board rose once again and hovered at the specified height.

Sin said nothing as he walked towards the house. The night-flyer simply turned and entered the building through an open door. Horizon got a good look at the tank containing the viscose slop he had used to bring down so many flyers. It was flatter and clearly molded to the shape of his back, unlike the bulky rucksack he was wearing. He would be glad to take this off.

104

His live connection to Rayo cut out as soon as he stepped into the old fashioned kitchen. It was an unexpected and unwanted wrinkle in their plans but how could one plan for the density of antique walls in a location so remote. Horizon walked through to the lounge, where he could see Sin waiting, and entered to find their host, Noel Lawrence, standing in the middle of the room.

"Do you like it?" Lawrence asked. "You were looking around. "It's been in my family for over two hundred years. It was an old drover's cottage. We expanded it, brought it up-to-date but not too much."

"It's not really my thing."

"Of course not." Lawrence sat down and invited Horizon to join him with a gesture towards an armchair opposite the sofa he occupied. Between the two was a low table whose magazines and coasters had been relocated to the floor. "May I have the diaries?"

Horizon pulled off the rucksack, stepped forward and deposited it on the coffee table before returning to his position by the wall. Sin watched everything from a corner of the room. Not speaking, barely moving.

"That's half of them, as we agreed once Tenku was in the air. The other half you get after you and I have concluded our business."

"Which you will be recording on those silly goggles." Lawrence smiled then leaned forward and unzipped the bulging carrier. "Was he a friend of yours or just a follower?"

"I've never met him before. He was foolish to try and break into your headquarters but he was only after the truth, like we all are. And flyers have no leader. You really don't understand us."

"You're a zealot, Horizon. You're not hard to understand."

"And you're a vain old man. I wish I'd known that earlier. Out there, they think your mission is saving the world, when all you really care about is your own legacy."

Lawrence paused his unloading of the rucksack to look up at Horizon. "You're assuming those are two separate things."

"You're deluded."

On the table, Lawrence arranged the books into three columns and then counted them, noting the dates on their spines. Thirty diaries detailing thirty years of his life; the first begun when he was a tender fifteen-years-old but already committed to making his mark on the world. These books were important, they mattered and not just to him.

"Was it you that intercepted my plane? There are engineers at Subah who tell me such a thing is impossible but my friend here," Lawrence nodded at Sin, "disagrees and I'm inclined to believe him.

"We found your snooping device. I assume it was through monitoring my correspondence you were led to these."

"I was only expecting a manuscript."

"Indeed. How your eyes must have lit up."

"I'm not interested in your private thoughts, Mr. Lawrence, only your actions. But I did look through your diary for 2040. Somehow you fail to mention air-boys falling out of the sky. Even once."

"And why would I do that?"

"Because you caused it." Horizon bellowed at him. "You tainted the dust and you released it knowing what we'd use it for and knowing what the result would be. The Fall. Air-boys dying, all over the world, and a wall of lies to protect Subah's name."

Lawrence observed the young flyer with something close to pity in his eyes. "You really believe that, don't you?"

"Stop lying. If you want to see the rest of your diaries, stop lying now and admit it."

"How can I be sure you will return my diaries?"

"You can be sure because I'm not the liar in this room. That's the difference between us."

Lawrence turned to Sin. "Is that what it is?" Then back to Horizon. "If I thought you'd take it, I'd give you some advice: it's not enough simply to believe in a cause, however fervently. The purity of your faith isn't going to carry you to victory, not against men like me. Practical men."

Horizon took a deep breath to calm himself. "Why did you do it? Why did you taint the dust?"

"We didn't 'taint' it. We spent months working on that batch; modifying, testing and refining it to be sure it would do exactly what it did. What we created it to do."

He looked Lawrence in the eye. "Tell me everything."

"I can tell you, Horizon, but to understand what I tell you, you'll need to be prepared to face some truths you may not like. Are you sure you want that?"

"Tell me everything."

"As you wish.

"Vishal had many wonderful qualities but he wasn't a manager," Lawrence began. "That's why he brought me in. Together we built a factory and scaled-up production of C47 panels. And then expanded and scaled it up again. We were so focused on growth and on supplying our, ever enlarging, list of subscriber nations it was years before we realized our Subah had a shadow."

"The residue black market."

Lawrence laughed. "It wasn't a black market. It was a nascent global mafia trading exclusively in C47 waste. Dust, as you call it. Our disposal procedures had been utterly compromised by criminal organizations and state agencies. We were pretty sure the old Petro Cartel had a couple of spies in there too.

"The deeper we delved the worse it got. We began to hear rumors of energy weapons in development, C47 powered tanks and drones that could remain in the air indefinitely. The most important invention of the twenty-first century, our dream to bring light and heat to everyone, was being perverted into just another way to spread fear and violence.

"And we could do nothing. To halt production would have been to endanger the revolution we had started. You're too young to understand how much opposition we faced in those early years. Nothing was certain. We needed time to re-engineer and upgrade our manufacturing operation. I came to the conclusion that the only sure way to do that was to kill demand.

"After we allowed the modified waste to feed into the underground channels, that's exactly what happened. It gave us the breathing space we needed." Lawrence sat back on the sofa waiting for the question he knew was coming.

"What about the air-boys?"

"What your air-boys received were the scraps of the scraps. They were benefiting from corruption within an already illegal supply chain, small players trying to do a little business for themselves on the side. The chain didn't exist for them.

"You weren't our target, Horizon."

"We weren't your target? Air-boys fell from the sky. They fell from the sky because of your bad dust but we weren't your target?"

Lawrence looked at him and this time Horizon was sure it was pity in his eyes. "You weren't even an afterthought."

He had waited so long. He had anticipated and imagined the moment when Subah would finally acknowledge their culpability so many times and, now it was here, Horizon felt lightheaded. He reached out to the wall behind him to steady himself and then he heard a new voice.

"It's such a dull pain, isn't it? That ache one feels confronted with a historic wrong long past righting. And you've been carrying it around all this time, haven't you, Horizon. The burden's warped you. You're crooked and bent.

"Call in your friend. Leave the diaries and your goggles and you can both go, I give you my word. It's the best way this ends. We both know that beaten up old Sun-Jammer doesn't stand a chance against my board."

"You should listen to him." Lawrence counseled. "Clearly, this isn't the story you were expecting."

"I've got some advice for you," Horizon countered. "If you think causing dozens of deaths through negligence rather than malice will spare Subah's reputation, you're very wrong.

"Who else knows about this?"

"We told the governments we needed to tell. They chose not to share the information with their citizens. Likely, because they were the ones responsible for the very espionage that precipitated our action but also, I dare venture, because they understood my decision. It was right then and it's right now."

"If you're so sure of that, why leave it out of your diaries?" Lawrence was silent and Horizon observed the discomfort his question had provoked play out on the old man's face. Such silence was an unnatural state for someone so taken with the sound of their own voice. "That's what I thought."

"I've told you what you wanted to know." Lawrence snapped. "Return the rest of my property. That was our agreement."

"I'll need to step outside."

"Then I hope you won't be offended if my friend joins you."

Sin followed Horizon as he retraced his steps through the kitchen and out of the house where his flight-com immediately picked-up Rayo.

"Harm done. Bring the rest of them." He half-turned to Sin. "Is it back to the silent treatment?"

"You've heard my offer. It stands. Take it while you have the chance. I'm in no hurry to ground you and your friend."

"Oh… Because you'll catch-up with us eventually. Right?"

"You have no idea how hard it was to convince Subah to let me do this alone. They only agreed as a favor to Sir Lawrence. He wanted everything done quietly. You have a window of opportunity, you don't deserve, thanks to him.

"And 'yes,' I'll catch-up with all of you. You're a loose end that needs clipping."

Rayo appeared from behind the building, over their heads, and landed in the field beside the house. She sent up her board and walked towards them. Sin turned back into the property.

Horizon spoke quietly as Rayo drew near. "Old cottage. Thick walls. We're going to have to improvise." She answered with the slightest of nods and followed him inside.

On Rayo entering the front room, Noel Lawrence rose to his feet. It was a gesture that earned him only scorn from his newest visitor.

"Please… you're no gentleman to me. You're the man who tried to crush a movement and failed."

"A movement?" Lawrence repeated. "By which you mean, reckless youths building thrill-machines with stolen technology? That's one word for it."

"Do you have my diaries?"

Rayo took off the rucksack she was wearing and held it out to Lawrence who received it, eagerly, before returning to the sofa where he began removing the diaries, already stacked on the coffee table, to the floor. The exchange completed, Rayo looked over at Sin, in the corner of the room. He turned his black visor to face her.

"I might prefer the word 'delinquents' but I suppose it's a matter of perspective. What is in no doubt is that C47 was never created for you, my dear."

"Shouldn't we be asking Vishal Vohra that?" Horizon retorted. "Not his admin guy."

"Vishal Vohra is dead. He's been dead for ten years," Lawrence continued. "He was taken from his home by people who wanted the secret to manufacturing his compound; tortured by them and left to die. But he didn't tell them anything."

"How do you know that?"

"We know it now because, in the years since, no one has been able to successfully replicate C47. We knew it then because of the number of pieces we found him in.

"Unfortunately, we were never able to discover who it was that had taken him. One thing I was sure of, however; the world didn't want to hear this story." Lawrence lifted Rayo's bag onto the table and unzipped it. "Perhaps, young man, you're beginning to see why I'm so protective of the technology he created."

Horizon pointed at the man in the corner. "But you were happy to take our tech and pervert it. You built a militarized air-board to hunt us down."

"Your tech?"

"Air-boy tech."

"The air-boys are gone." Sin declared wearily.

"Then what are we?" Rayo asked.

"Remnants. Confused and a danger to yourselves. You're children playing in ruins."

Lawrence chuckled. "You're too harsh, my friend. I find their New World optimism charming." He began to unpack the second rucksack.

"Enough of this. Sin stepped forward. "By now the two of you must be wondering why your flight-coms still won't connect. That was your plan, right? Two flyers with two copies of the recording and only one me to chase you both down?

"It's because I'm jamming them. I got Subah to rig me up a portable version of the signal-suppressing tech they use on-site. Its range is a fraction of what they have at the factory but, Horizon; you'll never get far enough away from me to transmit anything. It's over."

Lawrence had built one stack of ten diaries and dipped into the bag for more. "You should listen to him. He's sparing you the fate of Cassandra, and who would want such…" Thick grey smoke exploded from the rucksack. In an instant, neither Lawrence, the bag nor the sofa were visible.

Rayo threw herself at Sin and, before he could react, landed a solid double-fisted punch on his jaw, knocking him off his feet. "That's for Polaris." She turned back to Horizon, "Go!" Before she too was lost in the smoke.

He sprinted through the darkening kitchen and out into the light. The fresh air never tasted so good and was never so needed if he was to keep his pace up. About twenty yards from the house his air-board's signal appeared on his goggle's display. By the time Sin had fought his way out behind him, Horizon was already in the air.

He didn't want to waste time gaining altitude in open country so once he had doubled the height of the highest trees, Horizon gunned his rotors, turning his board south-east towards London. He pushed his speed to the limit of what a Sun-Jammer could manage and held steady. He was free and airborne in a clear sky but his situation remained grim.

Sin was right. There was no way he could escape a Corvette and there was no help up here. Assuming Rayo was back on her feet and her board hadn't been neutralized, she would never be able to reach him before Sin. But if he had lingered in the valley, while the odds would have been in their favor, the superior technology Subah had provided their operative with still gave him the edge. Horizon's only choice was to try and stay ahead of his pursuer and the only way he knew to achieve that was to disable the safety protocols on his air-board. He had done it without telling anyone. Just in case.

His flight-com's status indicator flashed and went offline, prompting him to look back. Sin was in the air behind him.

He was further away than Horizon had been from the house when he got his signal back, which suggested either the old building's walls had some limiting effect on Subah's jamming tech or Sin had just had it turned down earlier. Neither circumstance presented any practical advantage he could see or might utilize in his current situation and he was running out of time to find something, anything that might provide him with an alternative to the one course he had because Sin was gaining on him. He was gaining on him, fast.

Without warning, his comms came back online and Horizon heard a voice. "Stand down. You can't get away and you can't broadcast unless I let you. End this now before we both do something we may regret."

Horizon took a moment to look around. Perfect blue overhead and fields and woods of green beneath him. If he'd had the chance to pick a day to be chased across the sky, a day for one final flight, it would have looked like this. A warning flashed up on his goggles as he increased power to the air-board's rotors, cycling them beyond the spindizzy's ability to synchronize, and hurling him forward.

He needed to reach London. Imp, Greenray and the two British flyers Imp had made contact with were there and the only help he could expect. If Rayo had made it out of the valley, she would have contacted them and told them he was on his way. Only together they might stand a chance against Sin. But he needed to get there first.

The voice returned in his ear-piece. "Horizon, you've pushed your board too far, your spindizzy's cracked. Land now." There was concern in Sin's tone, something he had not been expecting. "I recognize that air-board you're riding. Listen to me, Brink wouldn't want this."

He saw a grouping of reservoirs up ahead. As they raced by beneath him, Horizon yanked his flight-com free and tossed it into one of the man-made lakes. There was no stopping and there was no turning back; all he felt was the wind on his face and the tingle that had started in his feet. It was a new sensation, not painful, not yet, but, over the course of the next hour, it would creep further and further up his legs while morphing into a strange numbness that made it difficult to remain in control of his board. As he approached the capital, the effort and concentration required to stay on course had exhausted him.

He was so fatigued, at first he wouldn't believe his eyes, when he saw them. He kept looking and waiting for what he assumed was a mirage to fade but it only got bigger. A dozen, perhaps more, flyers, static on their air-boards in the sky ahead of him and holding position on the edge of the city. A wall in the sky. His smart-goggles picked out and magnified a few of the closest. Some were wearing suits while others looked like they had jumped out of bed, dusted off their boards and taken to the air, as they were. He had never seen so many together in one place.

He looked back over his shoulder. Sin had stopped chasing him. The feared night-flyer who had told him earlier that day that it was 'over' now hovered at the city limits watching him escape.

He turned front and allowed himself a smile before easing up on his speed and almost passing out. His body felt like it was on fire and a confused second later he realized he was tumbling toward the ground. He fought to stay conscious and regain control of the air-board but his legs would not respond and his vision was dissolving into a fizzing black nothing. The last thing Horizon remembered before it closed in completely was Imp's voice.

"We've got you, buddy."

*   *   *   *   *

When the boneyard found out she had connections within the flyer community they stopped co-operating with the FBI and told them they had no interest in seeing Gillian prosecuted. She might have got away with the entire thing if the Bureau hadn't decided to drop in on her employers. Once management at the store found out she was not sick in bed but on a jaunt back to Phoenix for reasons that remained obscure, they fired her. The news left her, surprisingly, unmoved.

On her return to New York, however, she discovered that her dismissal had not been met with universal equanimity. While clearing out her locker, a now ex co-worker told Gillian that Brendan had gone ballistic and marched into the office to demand their boss either rehire her or face his immediate departure in protest. They had accepted his resignation on the spot. The next day she sat with him in a coffee shop, listening to a less colorful version of the story.

He suggested she move in with him as they were both out of work and it would save her a lot of money. Gillian declined and suggested he not rule out selling his house and finding a nice apartment, reminding him that he only had a high school diploma to fall back on and how long both of them had been off the job market. She left him ruminating. As sweet as Brendan was, she was not sure their relationship would survive the transition their lives were experiencing.

Gillian began her pursuit of a new position at a leisurely pace. The truth was she was enjoying not having a schedule and, she told herself, she would ramp up her efforts organically as the days progressed. This had yet to happen the morning her phone woke her up and a breathless Miguel, calling from a detention center, told her to switch on the TV. Overnight, a gathering of flyers, in numbers not seen in a decade, had been observed over London. Global news networks were captivated but had nothing to share with their viewers beyond blurry footage shot from street level by witnesses.

Within the depths of the dark-web, the smattering of rough websites and ancient forums that constituted the flyer community online were already abuzz. Gillian pored over their updates of events in London and the condition of Horizon and her heart sank.

* * * * *

Cameron's auto maneuvered itself into one of the bays and unlocked its doors. He stepped out into a welcome coolness carrying the unmistakable taste of the ocean on its breeze. He couldn't see it but he welcomed its presence and the tempering effect it had on Long Beach's climate after two weeks inland trying and, mostly, failing to acclimatize.

He crossed the auto park to the hospital's entrance holding his phone. Within the device were the ward and room number of the stranger he had come to visit. A man he had never met who had, nevertheless, had such a big effect on his life. One that left him looking at the world so very differently and unsure of the path he had, up to this point, intended to follow. When he knocked at the door, instead of a call to either enter or depart, it opened and a familiar face looked out at him.

"What are you doing here?" Rayo asked. "Come in but keep it down, he's sleeping."

Cameron entered the room while she closed the door behind him. There was a muted TV in a bracket on the wall and, across from it, a young man asleep in a bed. Alongside him was a chair with a book open on its seat.

"This is Horizon?" Cameron whispered.

"You don't need to whisper. And call him 'Ben.' He's not a flyer anymore." Rayo walked past him to stand beside the bed. "Why are you here? And how did you know I would be?"

Cameron pulled out the Polaroid and handed it to Rayo.

"I emailed Gillian Tapp. I wanted to post it to her but, when she found out I was in Vegas, she told me to bring it here. You know she's taken down Skyline? It's just gone."

Rayo was silent. She seemed lost in the photograph which she cupped in both hands as if she were cradling a relic. Mesmerized.

"I found it at the same time as I found that air-board. I recognized Miguel and I'm guessing the girl is Sprite. Her and the old New York crew he talked about. It's hard to tell because they're all in, well, normal clothing."

Rayo carried the Polaroid over to the chair and took up her book, closing it around the photograph before returning it to the seat.

"Thank you."

Cameron shrugged. "It belongs with you guys."

"Why were you in Las Vegas?"

"I'm working there. I've got a job in a distribution center. They call it 'quality control' but, really, it's just keeping an eye on the robots. The pay's not great but it's okay. Still getting used to the weather."

"But why Vegas?"

"I needed to get out of Connecticut," Cameron sighed. "So I bought a cheap first-gen auto and came out west. I wanted a change. Maybe just for the summer, maybe for longer, I'm not sure yet."

Halfway through his answer, Cameron saw Rayo's eyes leave him and fix on something behind his back. He turned to find the TV displaying the interior of some ornate building. "What's this?"

"Oxford in England. They're opening a new library. It's going to contain the Noel Lawrence Archive. All his papers and letters collected together."

Sure enough, as Cameron watched, a still image of Lawrence appeared across half of the screen. Rayo spoke again, this time in Spanish and, while the exact meaning of her words was lost on him, her feelings toward the man on the TV were plain enough. They rose along with her volume, prompting him to glance at the still sleeping occupant of the bed.

"Aren't you worried you'll wake him?"

"He's sedated. As long as we don't start shouting at each other we'll be fine."

"Why is he sedated?"

Rayo looked at him as if he had said something idiotic and then stepped closer to the bed and took hold of one corner of the covering quilt. She threw it back to reveal the bottom half of the sleeper and the two stumps where his legs should have been poking out from beneath his gown. Cameron heard himself swear, in English and loudly, and then felt a hand on his arm as he was marched backwards out of the room.

Outside, Rayo slotted her book into one of the pockets on her cargos. "You didn't know?"

"That the guy had, had his legs amputated? No." Cameron was still shaken. "How did it happen?"

"Walk with me. Come on." She moved off down the hospital's corridor. After a second to compose himself, Cameron followed. "Horizon took a risk he thought would improve our chances of success in the mission we had undertaken. It did."

"And was it worth it? Was it worth that?"

"You've spent a bit of time with us now; what do you think he would say?"

Cameron was sure he knew the answer to that question. It did not make him feel any better or reduce the horror of what he had just seen. "This mission, was it about the Subah Corporation and this recording that's supposed to be going around?"

"Have you seen it?"

"No. I've just read people talking about it online. They all say when they follow a link it's already been taken down."

"You should try and find it."

"Someone said Vishal Vohra is dead. That's crazy. I did a project on him in the sixth grade. He was my hero."

They had arrived at a bank of elevators where Rayo tried to hide her disappointment as she pressed for a cabin. "Do you remember what I told you in New York about Subah and what the air-boys believe?"

"Sure."

"Well, now we have proof."

"The video? Even if it was, and that's a big 'if,' what do you expect? Do you think people are going to run out and rip the panels from their roofs in disgust? That's not happening."

The elevator doors opened and they got in. Cameron noted that Rayo selected the topmost floor of the building. He should not be surprised, by now, that they were headed in different directions yet he still wanted to hear what she thought. The flyers, in their own way, were seductive. Their mastery of the air still had the power to inspire awe and their confidence in the face of the law; in the face of the Subah Corporation; in the face of danger, gave them a strength he found enviable even if he was certain it sometimes took them to places they ought not to go.

"I shouldn't tell you this," Rayo began. "My grandfather was in the military. But, when I was a child, I noticed he never used to go to the reunions or march in the parades. He never celebrated the national days or went to the memorials.

"When I was a little older I asked him why and he told me that, for him, they were all for show. That they were made up by politicians to pacify the people by making them think all the important battles had been won and that there was nothing left to fight for.

"He didn't believe that. He thought all the important victories, the ones that guaranteed our freedoms, our rights, were temporary; and that every new generation had to fight the same battles, all over again, not to move forward but just to stop slipping backwards.

"I agree with him."

"And what battle was this?" Cameron asked.

"It was the battle for truth."

The door to the roof had been wedged open with a small backpack. Sunlight, reflecting off the C47 outside, exploded through the opening causing Cameron to raise a hand to shield his eyes. Rayo dipped into a pocket for her smart-goggles and then stooped to recover her bag.

Breaking up the panels covering the hospital's roof were a landing pad and a pathway into the building. Rayo's air-board floated into view as soon as they stepped outside and came to a stop, a few inches above the ground, at her feet. She pulled on the backpack and turned back to Cameron.

"You've been our friend, even when you didn't know you were doing it, I appreciate that. And the board you returned to us has already been passed onto a new owner."

"Dust is a must."

Rayo smiled. "Yes it is. If you ever need our help, call on us."

"How?"

"I'm sure you'll find a way." She stepped onto the air-board and secured her feet. "You found me this time."

"Does this mean you're in charge now?"

Rayo began to float away, disappearing into the glare thrown up by the rooftops surface while she called back to him. "Flyers have no leader, Cameron."
